The main attraction of the cadet booth is Lloyd's service!

©Nao Watanuki

The Military Festival was made for love! He may not know he's on a date, but evil does!

[CONTENTS]

Suppose a **Kid** from the **Last** **Dungeon** **Boonies** moved to a **Starter** **Town**

9

Toshio Satou

Illustration by
Nao Watanuki

YEN ON
NEW YORK

Suppose a Kid from the LAST DUNGEON ⑨ BOONIES moved to a Starter Town

TOSHIO SATOU

Translation by Andrew Cunningham
Cover art by Nao Watanuki

TATOEBA LAST DUNGEON MAENO MURANO SHOUNEN GA JYOBAN NO MACHI
DE KURASUYOUNA MONOGATARI volume 9
Copyright © 2020 Toshio Satou
Illustrations copyright © 2020 Nao Watanuki
All rights reserved.

Original Japanese edition published in 2020 by SB Creative Corp.

This English edition is published by arrangement with SB Creative Corp., Tokyo, in care of Tuttle-Mori Agency, Inc., Tokyo.

English translation © 2022 by Yen Press, LLC

Yen On
150 West 30th Street, 19th Floor
New York, NY 10001

Visit us at yenpress.com · facebook.com/yenpress · twitter.com/yenpress
yenpress.tumblr.com · instagram.com/yenpress

First Yen On Edition: May 2022

Yen On is an imprint of Yen Press, LLC.
The Yen On name and logo are trademarks of Yen Press, LLC.

The publisher is not responsible for websites (or their content) that are not owned by the publisher.

Library of Congress Cataloging-in-Publication Data
Names: Satou, Toshio, author. | Watanuki, Nao, illustrator. | Cunningham, Andrew, 1979– translator.
Title: Suppose a kid from the last dungeon boonies moved to a starter town / Toshio Satou ; illustration by Nao Watanuki ; translation by Andrew Cunningham.
Other titles: Tatoeba last dungeon maeno murano shounen ga jyoban no machi de kurasuyouna. English
Description: First Yen On edition. | New York, NY : Yen ON, 2019–
Identifiers: LCCN 2019030186 | ISBN 9781975305666 (v. 1 ; trade paperback) |
  ISBN 9781975306236 (v. 2 ; trade paperback) | ISBN 9781975313043 (v. 3 ; trade paperback) |
  ISBN 9781975313296 (v. 4 ; trade paperback) | ISBN 9781975313319 (v. 5 ; trade paperback) |
  ISBN 9781975313333 (v. 6 ; trade paperback) | ISBN 9781975313357 (v. 7 ; trade paperback) |
  ISBN 9781975318475 (v. 8 ; trade paperback) | ISBN 9781975318499 (v. 9 ; trade paperback)
Subjects: CYAC: Adventure and adventurers—Fiction. | Self-esteem—Fiction.
Classification: LCC PZ7.1.S266 Tat 2019 | DDC [Fic]—dc23
LC record available at https://lccn.loc.gov/2019030186

ISBNs: 978-1-9753-1849-9 (paperback)
      978-1-9753-1850-5 (ebook)

10 9 8 7 6 5 4 3 2 1

LSC-C

Printed in the United States of America

Suppose a Kid from the Last Dungeon Boonies Moved to a Starter Town

Suppose There Was a Mid-Series Redesign

Character Profiles

Lloyd Belladonna

Boy raised in the town of legend. Finally getting some confidence?

Marie the Witch

Shopkeeper shrouded in mystery. Actually the princess of Azami.

Alka

Immortal chief from the town of legend. Dotes on Lloyd.

Selen Hemein

Saved from a curse by Lloyd. Madly in love with the man of her destiny.

Riho Flavin

Former skilled mercenary. Hoping Lloyd will lead her to fortune.

Phyllo Quinone

A martial artist in love with Lloyd. Finally realizing how she feels.

Micona Zol

Lloyd's senior at school. Head over heels for Marie.

Allan Lidocaine

Noble's son and follower of Lloyd. Some envy his meteoric rise.

©Nao Watanuki

Chrome Molybdenum

Former head guard, now re-enlisted. His students cause him constant headaches.

Choline Sterase

Upbeat academy teacher. Nursing a crush on Merthophan.

Merthophan Dextro

Former colonel of the Azami army. Currently an agricultural evangelist.

Mena Quinone

Phyllo's sister and an academy teacher. Also an actress.

Sardin Valyl-Tyrosine

King of Rokujou. Also Mena and Phyllo's father.

Ubi Quinone

Former Rokujou assassin. Actually the Quinone sisters' mother.

Shouma

Young man from Kunlun. Has great hopes for Lloyd's future.

Sou

A man made from runes. Fated to never die, grows despondent.

Zalko the Thief

A master thief, able to steal *anything*. His next target is...?

The classroom in the Azami Military Academy.

It was normally filled with promising cadets, the future of Azami—aiming to become the best soldiers possible, busying themselves with their studies, eating an early lunch when the teacher wasn't looking, or conserving energy with a power nap.

But today an unusual assembly had created an equally unusual vibe.

On the right side of the room were the fresh-faced first-years. On the left, the muscle-bound, aggressive second-years.

And in front of these two groups, at the blackboard—a boy and a girl.

Micona Zol, head of the second-years, collector of scowls and owner of a pair of blazer-busting boobs.

Lloyd Belladonna, a popular first-year with a face as adorable as his culinary skills were delectable.

His usual gentle smile had been replaced with a grim look, his hands tightly clasping the sleeves of his uniform. Why did he look so stressed?

"...If you're this tense already, Lloyd Belladonna, you'll never make it out alive." Micona spat her words like a ball-busting boss.

Lloyd could only bob his head like a new hire. "S-sorry."

"If you've got time to apologize, use it to put the problem on the board."

He apologized again and grabbed a piece of chalk. In rounded letters, he wrote *Military Festival Event*.

When he was done, Micona wheeled around to face the hall.

"Hands up, people!" she yelled. "The Military Festival is almost upon us! The honor of the entire cadet body rests on your ideas! Our planning prowess! Our enthusiasm! And our appeal! It's no secret that festival success can lead to primo placement upon graduation!"

The army's annual festival. This one was all about the glory of the nation's military, unlike the foundation-day celebration in the spring, which was a strictly orthodox affair.

While the latter's stalls were operated by civilian merchants, here the stalls were all run by army staff. For the duration of the festival, the military base would be open to the public, allowing them to see the cannons, carriages, and latest railroad tech. The army's marching band put on a parade, and citizens were allowed to mingle with soldiers of all ranks. If you've visited a self-defense force festival back in Japan, you probably have a pretty good idea of what it might look like.

For the military cadets, this was a chance to strut their stuff and earn the placement they'd been dreaming of. They were extremely enthusiastic about the prospect. Their mood had that unique quality of desperation specific to graduating seniors at a job fair.

"Take all this down, Lloyd Belladonna!"

"W-will do."

"A feeble reply! And you call yourself a soldier? …You're a disgrace to your armband!"

The armband in question designated Lloyd as head of the first-years. Micona's scathing riposte made him clutch it.

His general friendliness and earnest disposition had won people over, and he'd been chosen to represent his class. The decision was unanimous, and no one had raised any objections.

"Augh…they believe in me! I've gotta live up to it!"

This was *why* he was so stressed, like an athlete just appointed team captain.

"Regroup! No holding back, lay any and all opinions on me. Anyone?"

A hand shot up immediately—a metal one. "Can we just do nothing?"

"I know I said any and all, but not that one, Riho Flavin. Rejected!"

That was a completely fair response.

The beady-eyed girl with the mithril arm was a former mercenary and infamously unmotivated by anything that didn't pad her wallet. She was a girl true to her needs.

Once her fruitless sabotage had been summarily dispatched...

"Then just make it something simple," Riho said, leaning on one elbow and electing to nap through the rest of the meeting.

Micona's brow twitched, but she decided to blame Lloyd for it.

"She's one of yours," she growled. "Keep the first-years in check."

"R-Riho!" Lloyd stammered. "We could use your help."

"I'll do my share once you pick something. Don't worry."

His efforts just rolled off Riho.

"Ugh," Micona said. "Forget her! Next idea. Keep 'em coming!"

The next hand up belonged to an adorable blond—Selen.

"We should play it safe and stage my marriage to Sir Lloyd."

"How is that the safe choice? Absolutely not."

This girl was so in love with Lloyd she no longer lived in reality. We should probably cross out the word "yandere" in our dictionaries and just replace it with "Selen."

Naturally, Micona had nipped her proposal in the bud.

"Ah-ha-ha. Selen, please go easy on the jokes; that one's a bit much, even to ease the tension."

Lloyd was busy sweeping Selen's inappropriate comment under the rug, as if trying to defuse a tense meeting after a joke...except that joke was something unfunny, like the boss saying, "You're all fired!"

"Aww, Sir Lloyd! I meant every word."

That was a problem in itself. Would Lloyd ever realize her affections were genuine? Unlikely.

Selen was the daughter of a local lord, and her misbehavior always got the attention of the *other* genuine aristocrat in the room.

"Dammit, Belt Princess!" Allan roared. He was quite large, just like his voice. "Lloyd's representing us; don't make him come to regret it! Let him relax for once!"

"Says the man who's already had his wedding," Selen commented, sulking. "Has wedded bliss left you *that* relaxed?"

"You! Can't! Bring that up here!"

©Nao Watanuki

Allow me to explain. Allan might have had the face of a forty-year-old trucker, but one turn of events after another had led to his being honored far beyond his actual merits. Poor thing.

They claimed he'd felled a dragon with a shout, summoned the heroes of yore, traveled to distant lands, and knocked the cap off a mountain with a practice swing. (All of these were actually Lloyd's fault.)

As his reputation grew ever more embellished, a series of particularly alarming mishaps had led to his meeting a woman named Renge—and a few days later, he'd found himself walking down the aisle with her.

Selen's accusation soon had him accosted by men who stood no chance at wedded bliss and women who couldn't help but be interested in any love story, even Allan's.

"This true, Allan?"

"I thought you were one of us!"

"Well, I never! With that ugly mug?!"

"Who is she? How much older?"

Lloyd, meanwhile, was looking very impressed. "Amazing, Allan. You tore down the barrier between the two classes in an instant! I could never do that."

"Probably for the best, Lloyd," Riho growled, not opening her eyes. Her role as resident snarkstress was never done.

"Okay, okay, table that topic for a later agenda," Micona yelled, clapping her hands. "Settle down, people!"

"Micona! I don't wanna be an agenda!" Allan wailed.

Lloyd had yet to write a single word on the board and was just awkwardly scratching his cheek.

"Focus! Ideas. Anyone got an actual...*hngg.*"

Micona's eyes had caught a raised hand at the edge of her vision. A very serious-looking girl beneath it.

"...Mm."

"Phyllo Quinone...has that been raised—?"

"...This whole time."

This tenacious hand-raiser was the silent, expressionless downer of a martial artist, Phyllo Quinone.

In the Ascorbic Domain, she'd mastered the art of the projectile chop, come to terms with her own past, and realized she had a crush on Lloyd—and had apparently polished her ability to go unnoticed.

"S-sorry. Please, speak."

Even the ever-haughty Micona felt suitably chagrined and ceded the floor.

"...Let's play it safe and have a tournament. With bookies."

"Does anyone here actually know what 'play it safe' means?"

Despite Micona's grumbling, Phyllo was already studiously listing the merits of her proposal.

"...Different payouts and odds for each entrant could advertise their skills to the world while also providing good training."

This plan came with specifics. It was clearly well thought out, and Micona found herself unable to dismiss it out of hand.

"I applaud the effort, Phyllo Quinone. However misapplied."

"......I worked on it all night...... I thought Lloyd would like it."

"O-oh," Selen said, rattled. "Well, training is good! I entirely sympathize with the need for constant self-improvement."

"...Makes me one step ahead of you," Phyllo growled.

"Oof! Phyllooo..."

By this point Riho was mussing her hair in frustration. "Geez, aggressive much? Ever since we got back from the Domain..."

Meanwhile, Lloyd looked thrilled to finally have something to write. "That's a legitimate suggestion, right? I can put it on the board?"

"The goal has merit, but we can't condone gambling. Not only will we face a mountain of paperwork, but we'll likely get posted to the fringes of the world."

"......Aww," Phyllo said, visibly deflating.

However valid, this series of rejections was making everyone feel like they were stuck. It was hard to propose anything now.

Hoping to turn things around, Lloyd changed tactics.

"What did they do last year?" he asked.

"An excellent question!" Micona said, immediately looking extremely conceited. "Heh-heh. Last year's event was unprecedented! Sensational! A program that had the masses shouting, 'Now *that's* our cadets!'"

"A what?" Riho asked, eyes half-opening, clearly certain this was nothing good.

"Brace yourself!" Micona cried, pointing at her. "We presented...our research on herbal remedies!"

A chorus of sympathy groans went up from the first-years.

With the exception of Micona, the second-years all looked miserable.

"Th-that certainly is surprising. Surprisingly pathetic."

The safest of safe bets. It was unclear what part of it could be deemed "sensational."

"If no better ideas are proposed, we'll be going with that again."

"You can't mean that, Micona!" Selen shrieked, yet Micona was serious.

"But I do. It did not earn rave reviews, but neither did it cause any harm."

"......Because no one came to see it." Phyllo was dropping facts, but Micona argued against *those*.

"Some people did! I interviewed a proper hardcore medicinal herb expert, so the presentation itself was filled with facts! I found it personally thrill—educational."

This was enough for everyone to work it out: *Oh, she just used this as an excuse to visit Marie.*

Micona was madly in love with a witch (and potion-seller) named Marie—who was the owner of the shop where Lloyd lived.

Trying to hide the fact, she got extra heated. "If there are no further ideas, we'll be presenting even more blissful research! I assure you, I'm only too happy to take care of it."

"That'd make things easy, but won't Colonel Chrome get ticked off?" Riho asked, flicking her half-lidded eyes toward the corner—where their instructor stood.

Would half-assing this not earn them his wrath? All eyes gathered on the man known for his fearsome drills...

"———Zzz."

And they found him flat out on his podium, mid-nap, drool running down his chin.

"A-are you okay, Colonel Chrome?" Lloyd said, running over.

Chrome blinked at him blearily. "Mm? Did you decide on something?"

"...He was legit out cold?"

Lloyd patted their teacher on the back, genuinely concerned. "Are you sure you're not sick?"

"No, no, Lloyd. Just...tired."

Too tired to even hide it.

This was extra alarming, and Allan ran over to join them. "D-did you eat something funny?"

Chrome finally registered their concern and awkwardly scratched his chin.

"See, the army's running this festival, so I haven't caught a break. Checking security, confirming event schedules, hosting our own event, acting as guards for international visitors, keeping the fine art displays under lock and key, and I'm sure the king'll come up with something horrifying at the last minute, so I've had nothing but quick naps for a while now."

He was way past mincing words. His students were left speechless.

"I—I see...the teachers have to put on an event, too? That's...rough."

"What are the faculty doing?" Selen asked, purely out of curiosity.

Chrome blinked a few times, then pulled a one-page document from his pocket.

"Rich with entertainment! Kind of an at-home theme park proposal."

Micona took the page from him and read it over.

"'Find Who's Hiding'? What?"

Chrome yawned into her frown. "Lots of wanted criminals who've gone into hiding, right? Dropped out of society. The plan is to get everyone to help us track 'em down and arrest them. If you've seen their faces, just say the word!"

"So...you're just handing out 'wanted' posters."

"A thing the army *already* does."

"...Lazy."

Chrome rubbed his eyes, not looking the least bit guilty.

"The bad guys love to blend into festivals and do crime. You all should remember these names, at least. Especially this Zalko the Thief—he's trouble."

He pulled a wanted poster from his pocket, showing it to everyone.

It featured a picture of a man running away, a painting on his back. His back was to the camera, and no physical details were apparent, making it utterly useless.

"…If you can't see the face…"

"Only photo we've got. And he's a master of disguise! So nobody even knows what he looks like."

"Zalko the Thief. Mostly steals precious art and valuables…" Chrome was absently rolling a bit of eye gunk between his fingertips. "Been real active lately. Trying to make a name for himself. Sending out calling cards and the like, begging for attention."

"A criminal who seeks fame, but hides his face? How odd."

"Just…be on the lookout. Bye!" Chrome tucked a pillow under his arm and headed for the door.

"Um, Colonel Chrome? We haven't settled anything yet."

"Hmm? But the king'll definitely be calling for me any minute— your entry can be, you know…whatever you want. We respect your independence. Long as it isn't *too* crazy, anything goes. And make sure you've got the security rotation set up. Make it good, Lloyd!"

And with that, he staggered off down the hall.

The door slammed behind him.

There was a long, uncomfortable silence.

The phrases "respect your independence" and "anything goes" looped through their minds.

A moment later, every boy in the room raised their hands, letting their animal instincts drive them.

"Lloyd! Put maid café on the board!"

"Lloyd! Maid hot pot!"

"Instant maids! Put it on the board, stat!"

The maid parade had him reeling, but Lloyd dutifully wrote every maid-themed suggestion down.

"Um…hot pot and…"

Fueled by desire, the flames burning in the temples of their minds, first- and second-year males blew the barrier between them to the farthest reaches of space.

But Micona and the girls weren't so easily swayed.

"Men! Why does it always come back to maids?!"

A phrase that silenced everyone.

But no matter how sound the objection, their passions would not die here! They had to fight, the consequences be damned!

"Nothing brings in the crowds like maids! Especially if Micona's boobs are involved!"

"It would *totally* be better than last year! Instead of revealing herbal remedies, reveal some cleavage!"

"You shut your mouth!"

It sounded like the second-year males had some latent frustration about their boring event from last year.

Micona had gone beet red and was yelling, but the sheer number of "boob" comments was clearly winning that fight.

"Riiiight, they all joined during the gear up for war with Jiou, so every second-year is a total meathead," Riho said.

The first-year girls all clapped their hands, eyes aglow with a new idea.

Meanwhile, the boys were still making arguments that probably wouldn't end well in court.

"It's a maid café! Between Micona's boobs and Lloyd's scrumptious snacks, we'll be the crown jewel of the whole festival."

"Hold up! You're backhand insulting maids now!" a second-year girl snapped, adjusting her glasses as she waded into the "debate." "The girls have a counterproposal! A butler café! Lloyd, put it on the board."

"Uh, okay…a butler café?"

The proposer's glasses gleamed, and she launched into an exuberant pitch.

"A butler café is—[fast-forward…]—in other words, exactly what every girl really wants."

Her twenty-minute tirade had every girl nodding, completely convinced.

"V-very informative."

"Then on the board it goes!"

When Lloyd had finished writing, the girl completed her pitch, her voice quiet—yet powerful.

"Lloyd's cooking will be the star of the café. And the butlers will be chiseled male cadets. And for customers of other persuasions—we can offer Micona's butch butler."

"Is that all I'm good for?!" Micona sobbed.

"And for our fiercest visitors, we can have Allan's topless butler. It is a flawless strategy, able to handle any and all comers. This festival is ours to conquer."

"What did *I* ever do?!" Allan wailed.

An assembly once divided between classes was now divided by gender, and the debate grew more furious.

Then Selen joined the fray.

"Sir Lloyd as a butler! Serving refreshments! That totally does it for me!"

"......Not an excuse to sidle up to him."

Selen would take the slightest excuse to snuggle up next to him, but Phyllo blocked her like a bouncer at an idol's meet and greet. They were made for each other.

But at this juncture, someone dropped a phrase that changed *everything*.

"But maids are better! Everyone loves 'em! And they make mad money!"

Money...makes the world go round.

Money...is the lure that captivated the hearts of all humankind.

"Mad...*money*?!" Riho's head shot up, ears twitching. She began pelting the speaker with questions like a reporter sniffing out a scoop. "Hmm? We're allowed to turn a profit? How much? What's our take-home amount? Grounds fees? Hours of operation? And..."

Overwhelmed, Micona pulled the manual out of her desk and handed it to Riho.

"I-it's all in here!"

Riho snatched it and did a skim, followed by a deep read. No trace of her earlier apathy remained. Clearly, she was living for this.

"No room fee...given our location...if we toe the lines of decency laws..."

Sparks exploding through her mind, she swiftly hit the podium.

"R-Riho?"

"Gimme that, Lloyd."

She grabbed the chalk like a boss and scrawled a huge circle around the words "maid café."

"Attenshuuuuuuuuuuuuun!!!" Her eyes flashed, and a hush fell over the room.

She cleared her throat and addressed the room at a more normal—but easily heard—volume.

"I, Riho Flavin, am here before you to propose the cadets' innovation—nay, revolution."

She acted like she was launching a new product line.

"Suddenly she's motivated," Selen whispered.

"...Must be money. Always is," Phyllo added.

"Merc!" Allan roared, stepping in. "Lloyd's head of our year! Don't you jump in!"

"I'm also in charge! Don't you forget about me, Allan Toin Lidocaine!" Micona roared, always sensitive to being overlooked.

Riho just put a finger to her lips, calling for silence. She knew how to control a room.

"Why am I getting scolded?" Micona grumbled.

"Don't worry," Riho said, her tone cajoling. "The innovation space I have in mind will let you shine like the blinding light you are."

Then she bowed—a movement so polished and graceful that Micona folded instantly, murmuring, "Well, in that case..." *Sucker.*

With her detractors silenced, Riho slapped her desk, drawing eyes back her way.

"Last year, the cadets displayed their research on herbs. A fine use of cadet resources. But unfortunately, somewhat lacking in popular appeal."

Riho wrote "attendance" and "engagement" on the board with the "nearly equal" symbol between.

"As you can see, failure to engage our audience's attention directly leads to a decline in foot traffic. No matter how information-rich the presentation itself may be."

"T-true...I'm proud of our work, but...nobody came." Even Micona admitted it.

"What it lacked was innovation! A good two tablespoons of it."

"......Is innovation a spice?"

Riho was unconsciously resorting to grifter tactics, spouting a bunch of things that *sounded* good in the hope of being convincing. Her friends were just shaking their heads, but everyone else was eating it up.

Well aware that she had their attention, she moved in for the finish.

"And what plan has the most innovation? Only one plan here—the maid café!"

She swung around, slamming her chalk into the board like that one cram schoolteacher loved by all.

"Ohhhhhhh!"

A cheer went up. Needless to say, every voice was deep and throaty.

"Wait a darn minute, Riho Flavin! Why should we have to do anything that lurid?"

"I've weighed a variety of concerns: locational assets, customer draw, friendliness factor...et cetera, et cetera."

"So money."

"Absolutely money."

"...Just money."

Correct! They know her well.

Riho's heart had long been replaced with money signs, and she could not fool her friends.

But however transparent her motivations, the men—especially those who had been shackled to the deathly dull event last year—were all fired up.

"Um, you mentioned the friendliness factor, but would a maid café really help with that?"

Even *Lloyd* thought these cadets were an unapproachable batch, regardless of the venue format.

Riho had seen this question coming and had an answer ready.

"Never fear, Lloyd. This plan is specifically designed to make the cadets appear as welcoming and hospitable as humanly possible."

She started drawing pictures on the board, clearly illustrating her plan. The figures she drew were grim military types and maids with sparkly eyes.

"Riho pulls all sorts of new skills out when there's a payout involved," Selen said, growing impressed despite herself.

Paying this no heed, Riho got extra heated with her presentation.

"As you can see! People assume soldiers are uptight! Scary! Grim-jawed! But if those soldiers are in maid uniforms? How strange! The surprise factor instantly makes them seem friendly. Ordinary civilians in maid clothes could never achieve this effect! I know this to be true."

"......What am I seeing, exactly?"

"Right, everyone?" Riho swung to the boy brigade for support and got it.

""""Damn straight!"""""

The cry was lusty in more ways than one.

"And one more thing! This requires both classes to work together! We have had our conflicts in the past, but here we will all wear the same uniform and be united!"

"Aren't our cadet uniforms close enough—gah!"

Riho's silent body blow took Allan down for the count. He did not look like he'd be getting up again soon.

"Maid clothes! To unite the world! With the first-year head providing home cooking! And the second-year Micona here providing boobs! The two shall be bonded in fraternity!"

"My bust is not a symbol of togetherness!"

"Don't be ashamed, Micona! With your curves, a maid café will make you and your gazongas into superstars!"

"You get way cruder when there's profit in it."

The men were drowning them out, but Micona was not the only girl objecting.

The savvy-looking girl with the glasses made her case.

"Given the prevailing cultural winds, we'll face a mountain of complaints from female customers. How do you plan to address that, Riho?"

But loot made her loquacious, and Riho had an answer ready even as she acknowledged the concern with a nod. A skilled manipulator knew never to deny an argument outright.

"Naturally, I have that covered. The women will be in maid uniforms, and the men dressed as butlers. We'll be addressing the needs of male and female guests alike. A dual-wielding maid-and-butler buffet."

She made this sound like a compromise offer, but only the women would be scandalously clad.

"We're still getting the short end of the bargain…"

"Why not?! We'll be in butler clothes! You in maids'! We're even here!"

"Don't be ridiculous! Those are nothing alike!"

They were starting to scuffle, and Lloyd tugged at Riho's sleeve, looking for help.

"What do we do, Riho? They're about to brawl!"

"I figured this would happen… Time to use the ace up my sleeve."

"You have one?"

As if she'd known this would never settle things, she readied her next plan.

"Eyes up!" she yelled, focusing their attention once more. "Maid uniforms *can* be a bit sketchy, but don't worry, we'll be keeping the skirts nice and long."

She began drawing an elegant uniform on the board. A long skirt, with little skin exposed—nothing like the fetish wear the girls had been picturing. Cute and fashionable—anyone would want to try it out.

"W-well, maybe…"

Riho saw their guards go down and laid her ace on the table.

"And to even the score, we'll have some *men* dressed as maids."

She pulled Lloyd in close, clearly nominating him.

While the bulk of the male contingent were every bit as burly as Allan, putting Lloyd forward like this meant *he* dominated their perceptions of the male roles in this café.

Cunning.

The model matters. Even for a commercial advertising a plain T-shirt, a tall model would look fashionable—except once you got the same shirt on yourself, it wouldn't look half as good, but that went with the territory.

But using Lloyd as a shield, she implanted the idea that male maids would be like Lloyd in drag—and this proved super effective.

""""Oh...""""

The girls' minds filled with visions of cute boy maids, and they had no mental capacity left to realize that everyone else here was basically a shaved ape.

""""I'm in!""""

The glasses girl pushed up her frames again, sounding *very* excited. She, too, was fundamentally a meathead.

All the girls in opposition flipped positions like Othello pieces. Everything else was easy.

"Better than anything about herbs."

"I wanted to wear something cute!"

"Think of the ships! The ships!"

One seemed to have ulterior motives, but never mind.

Naturally, in Riho's mind, she had no intention of letting any males besides Lloyd out on the floor. They would be trapped in the kitchen the whole time. Any skilled restaurateur knew to rid herself of anything that would damage the bottom line.

"Um, I have to wear maid clothes?" Lloyd asked, baffled.

But the enthusiasm around him was winning out.

"I'd love to see that! Oh! The sooner the better!"

"...Argh, same here!"

Selen and Phyllo had fallen for the bait.

And Allan was still out cold.

The only one left against the idea was Micona.

"Stop! Riho Flavin, I have not consented to this maid garb."

The mercenary knew right away that she was only objecting to Lloyd in drag. It was time for her final trick.

"Flip the idea, Micona. This is your chance to defeat him."

"Mm? How so?"

With a wicked grin, Riho leaned in, whispering in Micona's ear. "This maid-and-butler café will let clients choose their server to earn a commission."

That sounded instantly ominous, and Micona's frown deepened, but Riho had expected that and didn't let it daunt her.

©Nao Watanuki

"A beautiful woman like you would never lose to a boy in drag. You have two big advantages over him."

"Hmm. Certainly his appeal would be rather niche."

Micona was enjoying the flattery. She was never a hard girl to read.

And despite what she was saying, Riho was secretly dead certain Lloyd would be far more popular. She had a nose for these things; it was bound to come true.

But unaware of this, Micona was giving the idea serious consideration.

Lloyd had made her drink bitter tonic on many an occasion, and this was her chance to turn the tables. And an impressive showing from the second-years would give them better placements upon graduation.

If they were both dressed as maids, she was all woman, but he was cross-dressing—and that seemed like a clear advantage.

And if they tracked the requests, the records would prove her triumph in no uncertain terms.

"My path to victory is clear," Micona said, grinning. She turned to face the room. "Listen up! The cadets will be entering with this maid-and-butler café concept. I trust there is no disagreement. Put your backs into it! Let's make it a good one."

Seeing her fired up and taking charge, Riho grinned, muttering "Sucker" under her breath.

The idea of seeing Lloyd dressed as a maid *and* a butler had Selen in second heaven.

But the cursed belt on her waist—Vritra—was stretching out to check on the unconscious Allan.

"Ahem. Rouse yourself, Surtr…I mean, Tony."

Vritra tapped Allan's ax, and a pale glow appeared around it.

"——mm…morning, Vritra. Wait…Director Ishikura."

"Are you quite well? Few love maid cafés like you, so I found your silence troubling."

"That's quite a presumption on your part, Director. Okay, sure, I *do* love 'em, but…"

Time for a much-needed explanation. Allan's ax was possessed by the demon lord Surtr, normally shaped like a turtle on fire. During the incident in the Domain, he and Allan had grown quite close.

Meanwhile, Vritra was the former guardian beast of Kunlun. When his body disintegrated, he was forced to possess Selen's belt—conveniently made from a section of his own skin. She was now his lord and mistress and worked him till his buckles were raw, poor fellow.

Both were former humans, staff at the Cordelia Research Institute. Currently, they were trying to work out how the world had gone all fantasy, and they were trying to stop Eug, a fellow researcher presently up to no good.

"Then what? You're no longer spending so much time in unscrupulous clubs that you're nodding off in meetings."

Vritra had spent a lot of time scolding his subordinates in his former life.

"Nah, man, not that. You might possess a belt made of your own skin, Director, but I'm in some random ax. It's hardly a flawless possession, and I feel pretty out of it a lot of the time."

"Hmm. Well, hang in there. Alka and I will need your help figuring out how the world turned out like this and putting it back the way it once was."

"I know…yet here we are, putting on a festival, huh? Does nobody care what crazy crap our Lady Eung is up to?"

Surtr knew Eug's wiles were an active threat, but Vritra just used his buckle like a head, shaking it.

"That's a problem for Cordelia researchers. I'd rather not get these kids involved at all…but the other side seems to have deep connections to them, so perhaps it's unavoidable."

"Little Lloyd's a brother figure, for one."

"But until that day comes, I intend to treasure my mistress Selen and her school friends. As I failed to treasure my own daughter."

Vritra was watching over the cadets like a proud papa.

"Cool, Director. So wait, this maid café thing's a go? This world's got some mad Japanese flair…" Surtr was panting heavily.

"Try not to get *too* carried away," Vritra said, like a put-upon boss worn out by his problem subordinate.

And so the cadets began work on their maid-and-butler café…little realizing this festival attraction would be at the center of Azami's latest crisis.

*   *   *

In the audience chamber in the Azami castle…His Majesty Luke This-tle Azami sat upon a splendid throne. With him were Colonel Choline Sterase—her accent in full flair—and her best buddy, Phyllo's elder sister, Mena Quinone.

Chrome was kneeling before him.

"Chrome Molybdenum, at your service."

He'd managed to shake off his sleepy daze—clearly, he needed to be awake for this.

Mena turned her heavy-lidded eyes toward him.

"They say ten or fifteen minutes of sleep can kick your brain into action! Even business tycoons are taking naps these days!"

"*Hngg…* Mena, what's your point?"

"We can see the mark on your cheek, Chrome." Choline sighed.

His power nap exposed, Chrome's face flushed. "N-no, Your Majesty, this is merely…"

"No matter," the king assured him, stroking his beard. "Preparations for the Military Festival will be wearing you out, I'm sure. You are vital to the future of our army. Rest when you can, please."

"Y-you honor me," Chrome stammered, bowing deeply.

His generous ruler put a hand on his shoulder. "I want the Mili-tary Festival to end safely—especially since the foundation-day events ended in ruination by my own hand, albeit possessed by a demon lord. I'm counting on you to make that happen, Chrome."

"Yes, Your Majesty."

"Incidentally, where have we stored the statue Profen sent us?"

"Secure in the basement treasure room," Mena said. "It's a pretty big hunk of rock, so we figured that was the best place for it."

The king nodded. "We'll have to keep that safe as well. King Eve was most reluctant to lend it to us."

"You got it!" Mena exclaimed, fake saluting.

"Your Majesty, I helped haul the thing," Choline said. "But…what's it a statue of?"

"Oh, right, right! I was wondering the same thing. Fill us in, King!"

The king grinned. "Neither of you got a look?"

"It was wrapped in cloth to keep it from harm."

"Aha," the king said. "It's Profen's fabled Statue of Love."

"Love?"

"Love! It's a rather abstract piece, representing the god of amor. It's said that prayers to it will bring romance your way."

That certainly brought out the dreamy side of Choline.

"It will…? Fascinating."

"Mm? What's this, Choline?" Mena said, leaning close, knowing full well whose face had crossed her friend's mind.

"N-nothing, Mena! Drop it. Y-Your Majesty, you said abstract, but specifically…what *does* it look like?"

An obvious deflection. Seeing both Chrome and Mena chuckling, Choline hissed. What else are friends for?

The king folded his arms, mulling over her question.

"Tough to explain. At a glance, you think, 'What *is* that thing?', but it harbors this overwhelming sense of chaos and destruction, and what is born from that could only be true love. It has that sort of *deep* vibe."

"Huh…that does sound deep. Like a well. Is this statue up to something?"

"Mena, you are very perceptive. I do indeed have a scheme in mind," the king said. He produced a piece of paper from his pocket.

Everyone leaned in. It was a handwritten proposal for something he'd called the Love Event.

The king and his bright ideas, Chrome thought, his countenance growing grim. What happened to the man so humbly honored a moment ago?

"I see that face, Chrome!" Mena smirked. "Glad you conserved your strength now?"

"No comment," he growled, making his square jaw even stonier.

Some things were best left unspoken.

"Ho-ho-ho!" The king chuckled. "This isn't anything to get your hackles raised about, I promise. We're simply going to have the Statue of Love on display and encourage visitors to ask each other on dates in front of it. All it needs is a bit of security and someone to run the event itself."

He made this sound simple, but all three of them were sweating profusely.

It's gonna be a madhouse!

Their thoughts were so perfectly in sync that if they were piloting mecha robots, they'd be ready to perform final fusion and fly the giant robot together.

But the king seemed oblivious to the fact that he was sowing seeds of war like a farmer sows crops in early spring.

"Could be trouble," Mena said. "Especially in Lloyd's vicinity... We should maybe step in."

"Your Majesty," Chrome attempted. "Why would you pitch something clearly designed to give us all aneury— Ahem. Headaches?"

Neither his words nor his expression concealed anything. The king shifted uncomfortably, but he decided honesty was the best policy.

"For...my daughter, Maria."

"The princess? How does it help her?"

"From what I've heard, she has a crush on a boy."

There was a trace of sadness in his voice.

Everyone else winced. It was Lloyd-centric after all.

"And I believe her desire to be with him is *why* she refuses to return to the castle! She fears a political marriage...but I miss her so!"

Unlike Chrome, he wasn't even *trying* to conceal anything. Choline ended up patting him on the back.

"Well, she is a grown woman..."

"If I had my druthers, I'd have this man stand before a cannon volley!"

"Perhaps you need to grow up a bit, Your Majesty," Mena chimed in, the edge of her lips twitching. "Cannons? That's pretty over-the-top! Ha-ha-ha!"

"But rumor has it this boy's a hero. Saved the festival when I was possessed. Chrome, is this true?"

Lloyd had mistaken the king for a drunk, cleaned his face with a *disenchant* rune, and freed him from the demon lord's control. He may have gotten it all wrong, but the facts still stood.

Chrome knew this and how Princess Maria felt, so he nodded. "Absolutely true."

"Oh," the king said. A grave look settled over him, as if he was about to declare war. "I've spoken to him a number of times. He always looked stressed but was a nice kid. And there's no denying he's earned it."

"Earned what?"

"The right to join the royal family."

This shocker hit Chrome so hard it petrified him. Lloyd? Royalty? That came out of nowhere!

"Uh…I suppose…that could happen one day…?"

"Your Majesty," Mena jumped in, her eyes wide to show how serious she was. "You're moving far too fast. He's just a cadet."

"Hence, the event that will allow them to share their feelings! Best to rip the bandage off sooner; it hurts less."

It seemed the king's real fear was that his daughter would nurse her crush for years, only to have it end in heartbreak. And if she decided to deal with that by skipping town entirely?! He couldn't stand thinking about it.

Basically, it was typical "dad of a teenager" stuff.

"Okay, point taken…"

"It's an opportunity. I have the power to force him and Maria together, but if the feelings aren't mutual, they won't live happily ever after. The sooner that's resolved, the better! I miss you, Maria! Come back to me!"

Given the king's intentions, and more importantly his own desire to see Marie and Lloyd get somewhere, Chrome was moved to get on board.

"Very well. Chrome Molybdenum, at your service. I'll do my best to convey your feelings to her."

"Et tu, Chrome?" Mena cried, caught off guard by this sudden about-face.

"Is there a problem, Mena?"

"Not…exactly. Not in so many words. Fine, I'll help, too."

Choline leaned in, squinting at her. "What ails you, Mena? Ohhh! You're thinking about Phyllo. She's mad for him, too!"

"R-right! But oh well! It's gonna be a super-fun romantic event! That's how the chips fall."

"Sorry to drag you into a royal problem," the king said, bowing his head.

"The royals—especially Princess Maria—are like family to me," Chrome assured him.

"It really helps, Chrome."

"See? Now that's all settled, no time for jibber-jabber. We got butt-loads to do...so get a move on!" Choline said, pushing the other two out of the room.

Once they were gone, the king muttered forlornly, "I suppose...that boy will be able to complement Maria... I wouldn't be opposed to welcoming him into the family."

He continued, "This boy will have to do. The Dragon Slayer, Allan Toin Lidocaine."

Uh-oh. Kind of a big thing to get wrong.

The king had lost all memories of the time he'd been possessed, and he bought into the army's current media campaign wholesale, assuming the rising star of the cadets must be the hero who'd saved him.

Such was the irony of a king being swayed by his own propaganda.

Confusing Allan and Lloyd was less the seed of chaos than a stick of dynamite. It could not end well.

But oblivious to this disaster, the king was busy muttering, "I must be steadfast! It's all for Azami!"

He was trying very hard to convince himself.

Back in the classroom...the cadets had moved on to the next topic: divvying up guard duty and break times.

"Ha-chooo!"

Allan's stupendous sneeze briefly made everyone turn and stare.

"What's this, Allan?" Riho smirked. "I thought idiots couldn't *catch* colds."

"I'm not an idiot, so I catch 'em now and then."

Phyllo slipped behind him, stifling her footsteps.

"...Someone *must* be—"

"R-right, Phyllo," Allan said, "gossiping about—"

"......planning to *murder* you."

"I'd prefer to sleep tonight, thanks!"

"...Too much attention on you...and they resent you for it. Perhaps the other local lords?"

Her quiet voice right behind him was genuinely unnerving.

"I didn't ask for *more* specifics!"

"That can't be true, Phyllo," Lloyd said. "I'm sure it's Renge."

"...Oh. Allan's *wife*."

This was not really helping. Allan would rather that nobody bring her up.

"L-Lloyd...can we not discuss...?"

Renge Audoc. Leader of the Ascorbic Domain's Audoc clan.

Anzu and her Kyounin clan had retained control of the Domain, but she and her axes had been a powerful challenge. A series of coincidences and leaped-to conclusions had led this tea-loving lady to fall head over heels for Allan.

They'd gotten so swept up in things, they'd held the marriage ceremony, bringing us here... So why *was* Allan back in Azami?

Leave that interrogation to our resident love master (self-appointed, clearly), Selen.

"Exactly! You held a wedding any woman would dream of, so why are you here flying solo? A real man would live with her back in the Domain...or bring her here!"

All of that actually made sense. Riho nodded.

"A rare moment of lucidity, Selen. Allan can't possibly argue with it!"

"I could understand making an exception if you were like Sir Lloyd and myself—madly in love, ready for a same-day ceremony at the drop of a hat but deliberately choosing to savor the extreme romance afforded only to students."

"You say one kind word..." Riho sighed. "And I've no idea what part of this is 'extreme.'"

Once Selen started ranting, everyone stopped listening.

Micona wrapped up her meeting and joined them.

"Your typical marriage blues?" she asked. "You married without dating long enough, and she's an older woman, so after the fact you lost your nerve and said, 'At least wait until I graduate!' I bet."

"That is uncannily accurate; please don't do that again."

A surprise wedding—while still in school—would be rough for any man.

"I—I did want to get married...just...the way it went down is giving me cold feet. I've got no complaints about her! Just...with all the misunderstandings, I want her to see me for who I really am."

He trailed off in a series of mumbles that Micona ignored, turning her attention to the others.

"Save the chatter for later. We've got the security roster settled, and now we have to figure out what the café's serving."

"No need to save it! We can just never mention this again."

Micona gave him a look of complete contempt.

"For a man who never shut up about getting a girlfriend or bride, you're being awfully pathetic. Any woman worth her salt would want to give you a piece of her mind. Right, Selen Hemein?"

"There's no escaping your fate."

Allan cowered from the hostility directed at him from every woman around. He was clearly on the hot seat here.

"Enough futile yammering. Any girls with a moment to spare, get yourself fitted for your maid clothes. You too, Lloyd Belladonna."

Lloyd hesitantly raised a hand. "Um, do I really have to wear that?"

He was still dragging his feet, but all the girls wanted this to happen, and they went into full-force persuasion mode.

"Well, yes! You're head of the first-years! You must."

"It'll lead directly to greater profits. Please, Lloyd!"

"...Mm! ...Mm!"

"Just do it, Lloyd." The bespectacled second-year had joined them. "And forge a new path for yourself!" She pushed her glasses up.

What path this might be was unclear, but it was likely strewn with rose petals.

Seeing Lloyd waver, Micona added a blow of her own.

"You have the right to refuse. But the second-years are abandoning all pride and doing everything they can to make the café a success. If you can't match their energy, feel free to take that armband off right here and now."

"Urp...I-I'll give it a whirl..."

He was representing his class—and that proved an exploitable weakness.

"That is the first time Micona has ever functioned like an upperclassman should."

"Fascinating choice of words, Riho Flavin."

Ignoring this, Riho slugged her arm around Lloyd's shoulder, grinning from ear to ear.

"Listen, Lloyd. You're our leader. If you act, everyone'll follow. The bonds of our entire class are depending on you."

"If I'm a maid, we all come together?"

This...wasn't exactly an orthodox way to bond.

And Riho had nothing on her mind but the bottom line. However forced the logic, if it got Lloyd on board, it was all good.

"Y-you're not alone, Lloyd!" Allan stammered. "If it eases your burden in any way, I would be glad to serve as your foil! Your comic relief! I, too, shall wear the maid—"

"Don't."

"All women loathe you. I oughtta *wrap* you in foil."

"...How would that ease anyone's burden? Make it make sense."

"When you all concentrate your fire, it really hits hard!"

Allan getting teased again pleased Riho to no end.

But Micona's hand clapped down upon her shoulder.

"No time for merriment, Riho Flavin. You've got to get fitted."

"Nah, I'm the owner!" Riho said. She'd had this answer locked and loaded. "And with this metal arm...I won't even fit through the sleeve."

Micona's smile was positively diabolical. She'd seen this one coming.

"A needless concern. The butler outfits might be rentals, but the male maids have theirs custom made."

"Huh? They are?! What about the budget?!"

Glasses girl did her glasses thing. "I know a girl who's into cosplay. A word in her ear and she was ready to do anything we wanted."

She looked so fired up everyone instantly knew she was talking about herself, not some fictitious friend.

"Point is!" Micona intoned. "You get me mixed up in this, I'm not letting *you* wriggle out. You agree, Lloyd Belladonna?"

"Y-yes! I give you my word as head of the first-years. All of us will help in any way we can! Even if it's a bit undignified."

"W-wait, Lloyd! Don't pull the rug out from—aughhhh!"

Selen's cursed belt had just snapped tight around Riho.

"Leggo, Selen!"

"This was your idea! Own it."

"Hurry along, Riho Flavin. We still have to report in for the events we're guarding and review the list of precautions. We've got a valuable statue on loan from Profen, so we can't let anything happen to it!"

Riho's screams faded as she was dragged into the fitting room.

"What's this about a Profen statue?" Lloyd asked.

Micona frowned. "I'd love to scold you for not knowing—but I know little about it myself. I'm told it's quite old, and the king personally asked for it, so its security is vital."

Allan stepped in—half undressed, getting his pecs measured.

"A statue like that could inspire the king to order a last-minute extra event and create a lot more work for all of—*ha-choo!*"

Another massive sneeze.

"…Your would-be assassin speaks again."

"Stop saying that! I'm sure taking my shirt off just gave me a chill!"

Jokes flew, and everyone had a good time.

But nobody yet realized there really was a plan afoot—and Allan really *was* the target.

Elsewhere…a room in the manor of a local lord.

A gaudy office was filled with bric-a-brac, all gilt and flash, each piece demanding so much attention that the room as a whole felt deeply uncoordinated.

It was, in a word, tawdry.

If the goal of the room was to inform everyone that the owner was nouveau riche, then it succeeded.

The third-floor room had a veranda attached.

Meant for enjoying the view, the veranda attached to this room seemed to have a vibe that would make anyone suspect it was actually used to sneer down at passing merchants and pedestrians.

Seated on the couch was a man every bit as glitzy as the decor. Everything he wore was clearly expensive, but if he went for a fashion check, they'd show him the door.

This middle-aged personification of new money was clearly not enjoying himself.

He was furiously twiddling his thumbs, staring fixedly at the man seated opposite.

"……"

The target of his glare was a thirty-something man in a low-brimmed hat, a scarf covering the lower half of his face.

On the small side, but sturdy, he had the air of a man who's been through the blender and come out stronger. It would undoubtedly take a lot to throw him off his stride.

He was leaning back in his seat, clearly savoring the softness of the cushioning.

"If you could provide a progress update?" the nobleman asked.

The man failed to respond.

"……"

The lord's fingers scrambled even further.

"Are you sure you can pull this off, Zalko?" he asked, the urgency rising in his tone. "We *must* destroy the Lidocaines."

Zalko merely shot him a derisive look from beneath the brim of his hat.

There was nothing distinctive about his eyes, but that look was clearly a taunt.

"Zalko! Are you listening?!"

"I am. Never try to rush a professional, Tramadol."

The hatted man spoke at last, his tone far too assured to use with an employer; this was the voice of a man who bowed to no one.

Tramadol let out a long sigh. "It's been a month," he said. "I don't think expecting interim reports is too much to ask."

"You agreed to leave the means to me. It's going well. What's the rush?"

The nobleman's fears came pouring out. "The Lidocaines are so prominent that people are acting like they speak for all the local lords. How did a group of lumbermen ever come this far...?"

"That's hardly new."

Tramadol made a fist, pounding the table.

"And now they're joining forces with the Hemeins—who are busy constructing canals and paving trade routes. I was certain they loathed each other! At this rate, they'll be in charge for generations to come."

"Not my business." Zalko shrugged. These were clearly not issues that concerned him. "But I'll take your word for it."

"And if that weren't bad enough—I have no idea who they paid off, but his son's become the hope of the whole army! The people are assuming this Allan boy's the real deal! Appalling."

"I'd like to believe those hopes aren't legit. Stories about Allan Toin Lidocaine are all over town. Dragon Slayer. Meteors. Summoning heroes. Laughable nonsense, the babblings of children."

"I assume the Azami army are trying out some old-school propaganda. So transparent."

Tramadol was now chewing his nails, eyes unfocused. The ragged state of them made it clear just what a mess he was.

"I see. So that's why you hired me to steal their fame. Fascinating."

Zalko let out a low chuckle.

Tramadol stopped himself from biting more of his nails. "I'd hire an assassin if I could," he growled. "Getting rid of this Allan Toin Lidocaine... If it weren't for him... Heh-heh-heh..."

The swing from paranoia to wild laughter was downright disturbing. This was not a stable man.

Zalko uncrossed his legs and leaned over the desk, peering into his face.

"That I won't do. I'm a thief. I steal *things*, not lives. I've never stolen an aristocrat's honor before, and it felt like a challenge—that's why I took the job."

He took the job posting from his pocket, scanning it like a TV producer confident he's found the next breakout hit.

Tramadol scowled, flourishing his well-chewed nails.

"If you take pride in your work, then give your client peace of mind.

Tell me your plan! Or at least your progress. Look at these fingers! Have you no pity?"

"......You could try putting spicy mustard on them?"

"I tried that! It burned my tongue off at first, but I got used to it."

His client clearly meant this and finally earned himself a look of pity. But Zalko was almost certainly smirking under that mask.

"Heh-heh-heh, well, if I'm putting you in that state, I guess I've got no choice."

The thief scratched a cheek, relenting. Mirth was in his eyes.

"I'd prefer to wait till it's all over, then unveil the trick. More fun that way."

"Surprises have long since ceased to be fun."

"Have it your way," Zalko said. "I'm already burrowed into Azami, feeling things out, setting things up."

"For what?"

"If you must know...to kidnap the king."

"K-kidnap?! His Majesty?!"

Zalko clapped his hands together, clearly relishing this shock. "That's what I'm talking about! Well worth the effort to plan it."

"H-how does kidnapping the king lead to the Lidocaines' downfall?"

The thief nodded as if he'd been anticipating that question.

"During the Military Festival, the military band do that parade, right? The king'll be there. He's been out of commission a few years, so he wants to prove he's back in full health and has been advertising his attendance. I'm sure you've heard."

"I have..."

"Here we are, possibly on the brink of a dustup with Jiou. Imagine what would happen if he were kidnapped now. The seeds of distrust sown by the locust monsters during the foundation-day festival would sprout again. Everyone knows he'll be there, so they can't hide the kidnapping. The king's absence is guaranteed to arouse suspicion. The army will do everything they can to get him back...and will be prepared to accept nearly any demand we make."

"And where does Allan come in?"

Zalko chuckled, crossing his legs again. He explained his plan with broad gestures, like he was speaking to a whole crowd.

"We'll tell them if they want the king back, they've got to expel Allan and have the king himself tell everyone the boy's exploits were a lie. These are our conditions for his safe return."

"Oh!" Tramadol said. "I get it! Who cares about the fate of a lowly cadet when the king's safety is on the line! And the more meteoric his rise, the harder his fall! It'll be devastating. Heh-heh-heh. Clever."

"And without Azami itself blowing hot air up his ass, everyone'll know it was just PR bullshit, and the Lidocaine family prospects will be dim. That's my plan!"

The nobleman leaped to his feet, applauding.

"Magnificent, Zalko. I was right to hire you."

"Save the praise for once I've actually pulled it off."

Lip service to humility, but that was clearly a confident grin beneath the scarf.

"No, no, this secures my position. If the local lords can remain influential, that gives us leeway to deal with Jiou."

"Jiou? The empire?"

Was he putting his chips with the other side?

Tramadol was possibly getting carried away. He put his finger to his lips, explaining, "My family has had a long-standing, lucrative arrangement with the empire...in return for our cooperation when the war arrives. Which means we can't afford to have our influence here crumble. That Shouma fellow had terrifying eyes—he could sever our relationship and my throat anytime he chooses."

A shiver went down his spine, and he started chewing his nails again.

Zalko shot him a look of pity and rose to leave.

"Take care, then. I'll be on my way."

"I expect great things!" Tramadol called out, beaming once more.

Zalko left the garish office behind.

"Okay. Nothing personal, but life's about to turn on you, Allan."

The thief took another look at a photo of the man's ugly mug, then shoved it in his pocket, heading toward Azami.

*　　*　　*

Meanwhile, back in Marie's shop...

Marie was busily writing a letter as the dining room filled with the savory scents of evening.

Just then, a child's face popped out of nowhere, peering over her shoulder. The chief of Kunlun village, notorious kid grandma—Alka.

"Whatcha writing? A will? An IOU? An apology?"

"Why would I write any of those?"

"A will's the favorite, and the IOU's a long shot."

"Don't make the favorite the scariest one! I've got no intention of writing any of those, ever."

"Hmm? I can see putting off the first two, but being young means writing two apologies a week. I'm still writing them every time Pyrid loses it!"

Alka sounded dead serious, clearly meaning every word. Marie was left rubbing her temples.

"Aren't you the chief? And when were you ever young?"

"I used to turn heads every time I walked into a room... So seriously, whatcha writing?"

Marie showed her the page like she was brushing off a pesky child.

"Fine... I'm writing letters to everyone involved. The Ascorbic Domain, Rokujou Kingdom, invitations to the Military Festival."

"Ugh..."

"You asked! Don't act bored already."

Alka plopped herself down on a chair, all interest turning toward the meal Lloyd was cooking. All that nagging and she couldn't even fake a second of interest—a total three-year-old's power move.

"The army's in charge of this festival, so I'm doing my duty as the princess."

Marie might have looked like the spitting image of a witch, but she was actually Princess Maria in disguise. Having foiled the plot to overthrow her kingdom, she could have returned to the palace in style, but she wanted to keep living with Lloyd and avoid a political marriage, so she'd remained here. She loved Lloyd sooo much that—well, probably not nice to point fingers and laugh.

"Oh! Your duty! Gearing up to go back to the—"

"Nope!" Marie snapped. Then made a face. "Dad's still not entirely himself, so I'm helping where I can, trying to ease his burden. Without actually going back."

"Personally, I want you back so you can send Lloyd back to the village! He can still go to school from there! Now that I've got my powers back, I can just teleport him to and fro!"

"I'm not ever letting that happen!"

Annoyed by Marie's stubborn streak, Alka sketched a rune that inflicted a minor curse.

"Here, have a curse."

"Quit dropping weird runes on me... Augh, my leg just cramped up!"

"See? At full power, I can easily develop a rune that makes your leg cramp with uncanny timing. You could enjoy everyone around you going, 'You should exercise more!' or 'Stay hydrated!' So helpful."

"This damn curse! Owwww!"

Marie had stood up to protest, but sadly, the other leg cramped up, and she wound up face-planting on the table, taking the ink bottle with her.

"Augh, the ink!"

Her entire face was covered in it, like she'd fought a squid and lost. Without thinking, she grabbed the letter she'd been writing and tried to mop up with it.

"Oh...now I've gotta start over. Ugh." She looked dejected. Few things were more discouraging than almost finishing a document and having to start over. Really important documents never let you cross stuff out or make corrections, either.

"Aw, you're such a klutz. When did you change character traits to be fully cutesy?"

"Cutesy how?! And it's your fault!"

"Whaaat? I would *neeever*."

"Now who's being cutesy! At your age!"

Lloyd heard the ruckus and came dashing in from the kitchen.

"Ah! Marie. Look at you!"

Seeing the ink on her face, he went into full mom mode, grabbed a washcloth, and wiped it off for her.

"Did you get all flustered again?"

"Sorry, Lloyd. Augh! Careful with the nose! And my legs hurt too much to stand."

"Just behave! You're not a child anymore. Wait, are your legs cramped? I warned you to get more exercise…"

"No, no! It's kid grandma's faaault!"

"He's right: Grow upppp. Lloyd, is dinner readyyy?"

Who was the real child?

When Lloyd was sure Marie was cleaned up, he went back to the kitchen and started bringing food in.

He'd made a big omelet with rice in it, and a side of fried potatoes. Alka let out a gasp.

"Ohhh? Not often you make something this basic."

"Well, we're running a café during the Military Festival."

Today's dinner was a maid café classic staple, and he was practicing the dish and using Marie as a test subject.

"Aha! Well, it looks great. Lemme just dig in!"

"Oh, hold on a second. This café has a little trick we do when we serve it."

Lloyd took a spoonful of homemade ketchup and held it up like a pen.

"What should I write?"

"…L-Lloyd, are you…?"

"If you're drawing a blank, I could do 'To Chief Alka.' Let's go with that. Here!"

The ketchup soon formed nice cartoony letters. The omelet itself was cooked to perfection. Marie and Alka both stared at it, dumbfounded. They *knew*.

"This can only mean one thing," Marie whispered.

"Exactly! A maid café!" Alka muttered.

Yes, the primary dish maid cafés were known for. The ketchup thing only confirmed it.

The furious whispers continued.

"Wait, is Lloyd gonna be a maid?!"

"That'd be insane! I've gotta see that! I've gotta!"

"Don't say it twice! But I entirely agree…"

"Isn't it a military event, though? Would they even allow a maid café?"

"I singularly doubt Chrome approved of it. It's gotta be just some other weird café…"

"Good point. That was close! I almost lost it and started babbling, 'Maid Lloyd! Lemme see! Can I flip your skirt up?'"

The whisper party was making Lloyd anxious.

"Um, is something wrong? Did I mess up the omelet?"

"No, no, not at all."

"Yes, it's fine!"

They didn't want him suspecting their corrupt minds had run straight to maid Lloyd town, so they made a big show of taking a bite and going, ""Mmm. Looks good!""

It *was* good, and they polished it off in a matter of minutes and relaxed with a swig of tea.

"Well, if Lloyd's working a shop, I'm definitely blowing off fieldwork to come see him. Now I've got my powers back, it's a quick teleport anytime I want."

"Getting those back has just made you even more of a menace."

"All thanks to Satan! So glad he agreed to replace Vritra as Kunlun's guardian beast."

Satan. The demon lord of the night had once been captured by Eug, but after getting memories of his past back, he'd agreed to help Alka's side. His real name was Naruhiko Seta. He'd been hired by the lab a year before Alka, but she'd had him firmly under her thumb.

Lloyd looked up from the dishes at the name.

"How's Satan doing?"

"Just dandy. Fits right in! Still can't talk to girls, though."

"Ahhh…well, ask him if he can come to the festival!"

With that, Lloyd went back into the kitchen.

"He really looks up to Satan, hmm? The one man who's given the boy any confidence…"

"I heard!" Alka spluttered. "Lloyd didn't know he was a demon lord and asked for some training! And Satan thought Lloyd wanted to be his minion, so was happy to help! And the upshot of it was that Satan got his memories back! What a twist of fate."

"His memories? Of what?"

Alka took a long sip of tea and sighed dramatically. She did that old-person thing where they stare into the distance, letting the memories take over. Not what you'd expect from someone who'd *just* been fantasizing about flipping boys' skirts.

"I might tell you someday. How are Vritra and Surtr holding up?"

"The snake possessing Selen's belt, and the turtle in Allan's ax? They're swell. Surtr tries to hit on girls and Vritra scolds him for it… like a boss and his underling."

"That's what they were. I wish they could at least get back to human form like Seta did. If we could find the lab chief of Cordelia, we might actually get somewhere with the world and this mess with Eug. Where could she be?! I might have to get your help with her someday."

"Master? What are you muttering about?"

"Oh, nothing. As long as Surtr's staying under control. Anything else out of the ordinary?"

"Mm, well…there is something Lloyd said on the way back from that shrine in the Ascorbic Domain."

"Oh? What? What did Lloyd say? His secret love for me? These things slip out unconsciously. Love has many shapes and forms!"

"You're turning into Selen."

"I never! I was here first."

Not denying anything.

"Back to the point, he said something about meeting a strange woman in the bathroom."

"That hussy! How can this be allowed?! Who tries to look at people changing or relieving themselves?! She oughtta be set on fire."

"I'll get some oil. You can dump it on yourself and light a match."

"…I'll spare her that fate. A forehead flick will do."

Realizing she was talking about herself, Alka quickly downgraded the punishment.

And of course, it never occurred to Alka that this "hussy" was the very same Rien Cordelia that she and Eug were looking for. Also, not a hussy! Lloyd had simply borrowed the bathroom in the shelter she was hanging out in.

"Apparently, there isn't a bathroom in the shrine. But Lloyd swears there was…"

"That's terrifying."

And coming from an eldritch creature like Alka, that was saying a lot.

Alka wasn't in the mood for scary stories, so she turned her attention back to the festival.

"So what's this Military Festival all about? Is it fun?"

"Well…the army puts up some typical fair stalls, throws a parade, lets people touch cannons and weapons, ride army horses, show off the latest train cars, et cetera…"

"Mm-hmm."

"Also there's the king's top secret event, using a statue he borrowed from Profen."

"The king hosts secret events? Is it a secret even from his daughter?"

"Not really, no. My father…His Majesty is trying to do something romantic."

"Aha. An excuse to force you into a political marriage?"

"No, not that. I grabbed Chrome by his collar and made doubly sure."

Alka imagined her expression as she bodily manhandled her former guard and felt a brief pang of pity for the square-jawed soldier.

"He's in a tight spot… Also, what statue is this? It got history?"

"Seems like Profen only lets people see it every few years, a treasure only those in the know are aware of. The official title is the Akizuki Statue. I hear it's really avant-garde, but it shows the power of true love."

"Akizuki?!"

"Yes. They call it the Statue of Love. Supposedly, it blesses your prospects—"

That made Marie think a moment.

"Come to think of it, Chrome did say I should make sure to take Lloyd there with me. And if Dad thought of it…and Lloyd…and it blesses our union… No…"

Marie's mind hit on the idea that her father might be trying to push her and Lloyd together.

They'd lived together all this time but had not taken that final step… or the two or three steps before it. *This might be the chance to rectify that*, Marie thought—optimistically.

"Nice one, Dad. I'm in! Heh-heh. *Hurk.* Heh-heh-heh-heh…whoops."

Marie soon remembered her company and got it together.

She was here with Lloyd's personal love cop—er, love protector. Alka would never let this pass. What she was doing was like speeding right past a parked cop car.

Marie's eyes flicked toward Alka, fearful she might have picked up on it…but Alka had her chin in her hands, deep in thought.

"Wh-what's up, Master? You're rather quiet."

"Profen… The Akizuki Statue? Could it be…?"

She seemed to have entirely forgotten about Marie.

"My darkest hour… I've gotta be sure. Maybe steal it first…or destroy it!"

"W-wait, Master! What are we destroying? That sounds ominous!"

"Augh! Where'd you come from, Marie?! You scared the bejesus out of me!"

"You're the one scaring *me*! Nothing more terrifying than you whispering 'destroy' under your breath! What's going on?"

"Oh, nothing! Don't look at me like that, nosy witch! Or I'll add another little *misfortune* rune!"

"I'm not being nosy for—no! There's ink on the letters I finished! Augh, and on my face again!"

The *misfortune* rune had left ink spraying from her fountain pen all over the letters and her face. Once again, she was squided.

Lloyd saw the disaster unfold from the sink.

"What's got into you today, Marie? Argh, this again?"

He'd just finished washing and now had more things to wash—and he did his mom routine again, wiping her down.

"Thanks, Lloyd… No, let me do my own nose holes! *Honk! Honk!*"

He'd given her a full pig nose, and Alka shuddered visibly.

"I haven't used that since I got my powers back. It's a bit *too* nasty..."

Having your crush rummage through your nostrils...might be a reward for *some* people, but neither Marie nor Lloyd was into *that*.

"Whatever! Gotta get this thing back."

"Kid grandma! You'll pay for this!"

"Don't, Marie! Stay still! Your leg cramps—"

"Owwwww!"

"Argh, I've got the Jiou Empire, Eug's war jibber-jabber, and now this?!"

Alka took one last look at Marie's pig-nosed wailing and vanished into the closet.

In a castle room in said Jiou Empire...

Eug had taken control and was steadily building up military might—brainwashing handy civilians into helping with the war effort.

Her goal was to become the enemy of all mankind, forcing the world to develop faster. So if ministers or citizens abandoned their homes and fled, she did nothing. The country itself was growing quite chaotic.

Eug herself was sprawled on a couch, reading a newspaper. She had her helmet off, and her blue hair splayed down the back of her white lab coat. She looked like a young girl, but the vibe was totally "workaholic researcher."

She was the demon lord who'd ruled the dwarves, the secret right hand of the priestess of salvation—but she was clearly *very* human.

She read her way through the Jiou paper, then Azami's and Rokujou's papers, and when she was done, she just tossed them over her shoulder onto the floor. Someone's gonna step on those, slip, and fall.

"Criticism of the monarchy is mounting on a daily basis. Even the Jiou papers are just straight up announcing defections now. Nice! Makes it clear who's the villain."

Bored, Eug flung the last paper away, stretching. Lots of little pops came from her tiny frame.

"The more evil Jiou gets, the less they'll hesitate to use the unknown weapons I'm distributing. And once the empire falls, they'll turn on each other... In a century or two, we'll reach the science level of the 2000s."

And hybrid science-magic development would…

But before she could dream further, the door slammed open, and a suntanned young man burst in.

"Look at this, Sou! Such passion… Oh, he's not here."

"Indoor voices! What's up, Shouma?" Eug peeled herself off the couch, glaring at him.

Shouma was a Kunlun native and so devoted to Lloyd that he was hell-bent on turning him into a world-saving hero—to the point of aiding in the effort to make Jiou the archenemy.

Currently, his hands were full of colorful pamphlets, and his smile was full of teeth.

"Feast your eyes, Dr. Eug! Pamphlets for the Azami Military Festival. It's coming up soon! Wanna come with?"

"Hell no! Have you lost your mind? They're our enemies! We're about to wage war!"

But Eug's words went in one ear and out the other.

"They've got events galore!" Shouma gushed. "And it's the first festival since Lloyd became a cadet! Can't wait to see what his team does! I'm sure it'll be passionate!"

He was picturing Lloyd working the festival with such intensity he seemed high.

"You're a broken record," Eug growled. She quickly refocused on more pressing concerns. "Is the local lord thing going okay? That Allan kid's family is undermining them at every turn, but our plans hinge on them getting weapons to Azami and Rokujou."

Shouma scratched his head, his smile never wavering. "Honestly, not good! Tramadol himself insists he's got it handled, but if our backing can't help, we'll have to cut him loose. Just a question of whether we unleash a treant on him or use necromancy to zombify him."

"Ugh. Well, don't drag your heels on it. We'll need to work out an alternate import route."

As their conversation took a sinister turn, a third person entered.

"What's all this ruckus?" he asked, his voice as calm as Shouma's wasn't.

He was getting on in years, but he had a strange vibe to him—from one angle, he looked like a nobleman, from another, a merchant.

If he put on a uniform, you'd take him for a grizzled veteran; coveralls, and you'd assume he was a craftsman. He could be anything and everything, all depending on the mind of the beholder.

The sinister Sou. Created from runes to serve as the world's hero, he and his role should have faded from existence once the world was saved…but instead, he'd been trapped here.

He'd taken advantage of this to become emperor of Jiou—without anyone the wiser. Merely placing the crown upon his head and sitting on the throne was all it took for every human present to bow their heads.

"Ah-ha-ha! That is such a regal entrance!"

"I am technically royalty here. A role far less entertaining than I'd hoped. All I do is listen to the grumbling of all and sundry. I might as well be in customer service."

"Getting everyone geared up for war was a blast, though! And once Dr. Eug's weapons are done, we can sit back and enjoy the war itself."

Eug grimaced. "*Sorry,*" she said, clearly more bitter than apologetic. "They're still behind schedule."

Sou bowed his head to her. "We're counting on you, nonetheless. War will turn Lloyd into a true hero and eliminate my unstable being from this world."

The mention of Lloyd made Eug flinch.

"He's the one who destroyed all the weapons I was making!"

"He does that."

"I know! God damn it."

Every time, at the worst possible time, without the boy himself ever realizing it. Even thinking about it made Eug's head throb. Steam was coming out her ears.

But even as she went full puffer fish face, Shouma pulled out a video camera and started fussing with it.

"Such a shame! If we'd had cameras running, we could have made a propaganda reel. Lloyd, our hero, sensing danger, foils Dr. Eug's fiendish plan!"

"Save your pity for those poor weapons. If we don't get this war started, none of us will get what we want!"

"As the emperor of Jiou, I'll do my part. Manufacturing weapons to plunge the world into chaos is all yours, Eug."

"God!" she wailed, clearly well aware of this.

"Tell me, Shouma. Why were you raising such a commotion?" asked Sou.

He might be an unstable runeman, but he'd been playing this regal role for a while and had grown accustomed to speaking like he was in charge at all times.

"You're loving this part, huh? Take a look at this, Sou!" Shouma held up the pamphlet.

"Oh? The Military Festival? What about it?"

"If the army's running it, that means…"

Sou's face lit up. "It's a perfect chance to capture footage of Lloyd being adored by the masses!"

His majestic bearing was instantly replaced by "grandpa going to see his grandkid's recital" energy. Eug had been lying back on the couch, and she made a point of sliding off it onto the floor.

"I knew you'd get it, Sou! Passion!"

"That's not something you *should* get! Your Lloyd-love is downright creepy!"

Sou's smile never flickered. It was like he couldn't hear her insults, his enthusiasm definitely at "hardcore idol fan on the way to a concert" levels of fidgety.

"Delightful! The odds I'll no longer exist grow even greater."

Not a goal for everyone.

Casting aside the last of his dignity, Sou handed his crown to Eug, who sat up and took it from him.

"So we're off to film Lloyd's heroics. The rest is up to you!"

"Hah?! All of it?! I'm in charge of weaponry! And you just finished reassuring me you'd do your part as emperor!"

"That was a long time ago. The desire to go see Lloyd strut his stuff completely banished it from my memory."

"Do you think being honest makes this okay?!"

He was an open book, cheery as a child. Eug was on the verge of tears.

Shouma was already at the door, fully geared for a long journey.

"Come on… Wait, I don't need to rush *you*!"

"Not at all! Ruling is a useless job anyway! All you do is sit on a chair and nod."

Many monarchs would take exception to that.

Seeing them both headed for the door, Eug made one last-ditch effort.

"It's not useless! This is a critical juncture! Come back and— Augh!"

But as she ran after them, her foot slipped on a newspaper. Kids, make sure you put papers, magazines, and plastic folders safely away where they belong.

Eug went tumbling down, and the pages flew into the air above.

Neither man tried to help her. They simply waved.

"Take it from here, Eug!"

"Don't worry, we'll keep tinkering with the new demon lords."

Eug was forced to watch the two idiots leave through her tears.

"Everyone around me has the skills…so why do they have to be so *dumb*?" she muttered. The floor did not answer.

She meant not only Sou and Shouma—but her former friend, Alka.

A few days after this comedy skit in Jiou…

Military Festival prep was going well. The raucous sounds of the band practicing mingled with the hammers making the decor and Selen's full-throated yelling of Lloyd's name—oh, that last thing was unrelated to the festivities.

Prep work can be weirdly fun, and the days flew by.

They'd finished the arch the crowds would stream through. The romantic scene was set, and only the centerpiece statue remained to be set up—and the hour grew late.

In the treasure vault housing that very statue…secret government documents, gifts from neighboring countries, letters Marie had sent her father as a child…okay, some personal artifacts in here, but mostly very important stuff.

And at the center of it, an object as large as a man, covered in cloth—the matchmaking statue. It had been shipped here from Profen with plenty of padding to protect the more delicate sections, and that was all still bundled around it.

Across the room was a girl—bedecked in old-timey thief garb, a *karakusa*-patterned cloth on her back and a navy kerchief on her head.

Shpp! Shpp-pp! Alka sneaked closer.

Using all her superhuman powers, she'd slipped through security with speed and a little rune abuse to make herself momentarily invisible.

"Hokay, 'kay, 'kay. This is a piece of cake wrapped and ready to go."

Her criminal intent declared, she reached the target statue. Alka looked it over, nodding in recognition.

"That's the right size! I knew it. Best take a good look."

She ripped the padding off like a kid opening a big present.

Cushioning flew everywhere. The thick cloth flopped to the ground.

In mere seconds, the Statue of Love was completely exposed.

It possessed a unique aesthetic, like a man and a snake wound together, both smiling. The mere sight of it was unnerving. Sections of it could arguably be described as heart-shaped, but…less the Valentine's Day type than the type of hearts ripped out and offered up as sacrifices. Quite a grisly display.

Alka sat down, staring up at it, muttering to herself, lost in a sea of emotion, miming swirling a decanter of brandy with one hand.

"I was a fool, once. Making a memorial statue? I was almost always failing art."

She stepped closer, stroking it fondly.

"This snake is Vritra. He's too big, threw off the whole balance; I didn't know how to fit him in, so his proportions got all weird. That's on you, Vritra."

Clearly, *she* was not to blame. She reached for another section.

"It never does to overdo things. This was meant to be me! I wanted it to be tall and thin like I used to be, but somehow it ended up as a ten-head-tall monster."

She frowned, turning her eyes to the next part. It was vaguely humanoid, but it had a hat on that made it look like some relic from the Jomon period. She started laughing, despite herself.

"Bwah! That one's totally Eug. She was still cute then! When did she go so wrong…?"

Alka turned to the last humanoidish mass and sighed.

"Sou was still young. Not yet unstable."

She sighed once more, rubbing one of the scattered, unsettlingly heart-like decorations.

"…I used runes to make this, knowing he'd vanish in time. An expression of my affection. Acting like he was my own child. As a result…I blew my chance to destroy him myself, and he became a thing that can't quite die. Memories of the heroic Sou linger in the minds of the world, and my power is no longer enough to eliminate him."

Her heart was flooded with regrets.

"That said, I definitely don't want anyone seeing this piece of shit. Best I get it outta here… Hmm?"

She'd been about to teleport the statue out when she saw a gleaming blade in the corner—the Holy Sword pulled from its place in Nandin village.

"The Holy Sword!"

Smiling fondly, she stepped over to it, reaching out…

But her fingers passed through the hilt, like it was not even there.

"Still can't touch it. Frustrating, but at least that keeps it out of Eug's hands…which is a relief, I suppose."

Alka sighed, scratching her head.

"But how does that even work? If I ever find lab chief Cordelia, I'll have to ask. But no telling if she's even still alive."

Alka put her arms around the statue and teleported it away, using a crystal.

*　　*　　*

It was early morning, the day of the festival...

Not a cloud was in the sky as dawn broke. A beautiful day, perfect for a fair.

And though the sun had yet to show itself, beneath those pale skies, the soldiers were hard at work, doing last minute construction and performing final checks.

You could hear the band members tuning their instruments. They'd kick this whole thing off with a parade, and they were extremely fired up about it—and more than a little nervous.

Magnificent horses usually reserved for pulling VIP carriages were strutting their stuff, ready to join the parade or an equestrian exhibit.

Lloyd was devouring all these sights from a window, like a kid at Christmas.

"This is really something! Oh, is that where the statue goes? And those...must be cannons. Will they be firing blanks from them?"

Riho came up behind him.

She was definitely acting like she owned the place and gave him a pat on the shoulder.

"We're short on time, Lloyd! Food prep, decorations..."

"Sorry, Riho! It's all new to me."

Riho joined him, scanning the sights.

"I know! Damn, those carriages are using the *good* horses. That dapple-gray one would clean up at the tracks."

She was clearly getting a kick out of the festival air, too.

"This oughtta be fun for everyone...and that spells profit!"

In...her way.

"Hey! No slacking! Get to work!" Micona roared.

She was in fully lacy maid garb, snapping orders left and right, like a big shot manor's head maid.

"Micona's really rocking that," Riho muttered.

The glasses girl in charge of costumes had apparently had a tough time finding the right bust size.

"She's very pretty," Lloyd said. Such a nice boy.

But Micona took no pleasure in this. Indeed, it made her frown more. She was as she had always been.

"Don't try and get on my good side, Lloyd Belladonna. This is a competition, and I aim to win."

"Wait, it is? I thought we were cooperating."

"Ha! The second-years' reputation and placements are on the line. Just because we're running the shop together doesn't mean we're raising the white flag! This world is one of constant strife."

She dropped a declaration of war. With her, there was always a winner and a loser, no matter what they were actually doing.

"Cool, looking forward to it. If the customers are pleased and drop more moolah, it all works for me."

Riho was rubbing her hands together like a bureaucrat sucking up to an evil minister.

With a waft of floral perfume, Selen and Phyllo appeared—both dressed as maids.

"Well, Sir Lloyd?"

"...Too breezy. Not comfortable."

First, Selen. Glasses girl had her down as "Great potential, wears it well, just don't let her true colors show." Potential for what? That was unclear.

Next, Phyllo. Glasses girl had jotted this note: *Attempted to highlight the forged iron curves and nail all gazes to her.*

"You're both pretty!" Lloyd again.

"......Who is prettier?"

Phyllo had been quite aggressive lately.

"Er, um..." Lloyd didn't have an answer ready.

Micona didn't let him, either. "Don't stand around yammering, Lloyd Belladonna! Get changed."

"Er, um... Oh, right!" He leaped at the unintended help.

Phyllo gave her *such* a glare. "......"

"Yes, Phyllo Quinone?"

"...Nothing."

Riho was snickering the whole time.

"Her face sure is a lot easier to read these days," she said, like someone celebrating their little sister's growth.

"Wipe that smirk off your face, Riho Flavin. Your turn to change!"

"Wait, me? I'm doing duty as the owner, so…"

"And owners work the floor! It's a new age. Move! The rest of the boys are already changed!"

Micona pointed, and indeed…there were other maid boys.

"""" ………… """"

It was like staring into a mass grave. The boys' spirits had sagged so low it triggered the fail-safe. This was the result of that typical first-time drag thing—an initial belief of "I can totally pull this off!" followed quickly by a harsh dose of reality, a blow from which few can recover.

"Oof…"

Allan in particular was like spite personified. An assault on the eyes. A walking eyesore.

"Don't ever let him out of the kitchen," Riho hissed, like they'd encountered a horrible monster. "Not on the floor, not where human eyes can see him."

"Gotcha!" Glasses girl pushed up her frames.

She then took advantage of the shock to grab Riho's arm and yank her into the changing room.

"H-hey!"

"Don't worry, we've got it customized just for you. A good challenge! Lloyd, you take the room at the back. Don't let anyone peep—girl *or* boy. Come, Riho, let's turn you into a maid."

"No! It'll look awful!"

"Don't worry, merc, it'll be better than my look."

"That's too low a bar! You're already buried six feet under; it's not remotely reassuring!"

Allan's eyes were definitely dead, and his "help" unhelpful.

Once Riho was in, Lloyd was pushed into the room at the back, with full security setup (which was largely Selen-related).

Fifteen minutes later—after all, unfamiliar clothing took time—Riho finally emerged.

"The mechanical arm might be seen as a weakness, but if you specifically emphasize it, it pulls the whole look together."

"What does that even mean?"

©Nao Watanuki

"Potential is infinite." Glasses girl pushed up her frames.

"Who are you even trying to be?"

Riho's comebacks lacked their usual snap, and her cheeks were definitely red. She did not wear frilly skirts. Ever. Her legs were clamped together.

"Argh, dammit. My legs feel all wrong."

"I know, merc! There's a *breeze*."

Drag Allan nodded in sympathy, but Riho just glared at him, wanting nothing to do with this foul beast.

"Don't lump me in with you! Stay back!"

"……No jury would convict you."

No girl would want to be lumped in with a brute in bows.

Micona looked thoroughly pleased with all of this.

"Not half-bad, Riho Flavin! You look like the maid who gets things done."

"Miconaaa!"

But before anyone could lose their tempers…

A door opened. And the main dish arrived.

"S-sorry. I'm not used to this getup, so it took me forever."

Maid Lloyd stepped forth into the hall.

He had dainty ankles, so delicate-looking everyone present reflexively reached out to support him.

His flushed cheeks and tousled hair begged to be mussed by all, regardless of orientation or gender.

"Perfection."

Glasses girl performed a spectacle shove of triumph. What she had won was anyone's guess, but…Lloyd looked so good in maid clothes that anyone would declare victory.

"It looks so natural on him," no one was able to think. They just stopped and stared, enraptured.

As their minds caught up with the sight, they were forced to applaud. The noise grew steadily in volume until it boomed like thunder.

Lloyd was thoroughly baffled. But his confusion just added to the allure, and the applause grew even louder, with no signs of it ever stopping.

Only Micona managed to resist the urge, looking like she'd swallowed a bug.

"Hmph…don't think you've won yet."

She was resorting to clichés.

"I don't! What are we even fighting over? I thought this was a maid *and* butler café!"

Everything maid Lloyd said made sense, but glasses girl managed to turn her one gesture into a sorrowful one.

"I would love to feast my eyes on that as well, but the rental butler clothes have yet to arrive. They should be in a large box marked 'clothing.'"

"I haven't seen one… Did someone hide it?" Micona glared at the boys' side, wondering if it was a scheme to keep the girls out of butler outfits.

"I thought the same!" glasses girl said. "I already questioned them. It seems they really don't know."

The questioned men all seemed rather enthusiastic. Perhaps having maid Micona glare at them was opening the door to masochism.

"Well, I hate it, so make them all wear maid clothes, too."

"Will do!"

Glasses girl soon had the boys peeled and popped into maid gear. In the blink of an eye, they'd all become drag disasters, and their enthusiasm gave way to etiolation. No doors were opening to *this* fetish today.

"Th-then we're stuck like this?" Lloyd said, genuinely concerned.

Selen and Phyllo nodded in agreement.

"As much as I like the maid getup, I also want to see him in a butler uniform."

"…Agreed… Agreed!"

Their motives: ulterior.

The missing butler uniforms were a disappointment, but Lloyd decided to focus on making the café a success. He moved to the kitchen area, calling out.

"L-let's get this food prepped. Everyone, keep your hands moving!"

He was trying to act like the head of the first-years and motivate everyone, but the maid clothes rather undermined his efforts. The harder he cracked the whip, the more of a playful tap it became. But that worked on its own merits!

"Being motherly in this outfit… Lloyd's attack range is simply monstrous." Glasses push.

The way he scolded was definitely doing critical damage to several people present.

"Everyone's looped back around to 'reverence.' It looks too good, Sir Lloyd!"

"……Can I take him home?"

Meanwhile, Lloyd's beauty had put Riho back in her primary mode. She had her chin on her hand, speculating on the profits.

"We're gonna make money hand over fist. If no problems arise, we'll rake it in with a cherry on top. The haul oughtta be big enough to buy a whole house in some provincial area."

That "no problems" clause was a biggie, though.

But everyone here was too busy gaping at maid Lloyd to realize she'd just jinxed them all.

"That sure was a lot of clapping. Something to celebrate?"

A man was strolling through the teeming crowds of the military academy, dressed as cleaning staff, a hat pulled low over his eyes.

Those eyes might be unmemorable, but the way he carried himself gave it away—this was the thief, Zalko.

His plan involved slipping through the chaos of the morning preparations in disguise.

"Security goes on full alert once the festival begins and civilians are allowed in. It's far easier to infiltrate at this hour. Everyone's too busy to stop a random janitor and ask where he's going. Heh-heh-heh."

Zalko grinned, pleased he'd been right. The uniform didn't *quite* fit him, and that was clearly bothering him, but mostly he seemed to be looking for something.

"This janitorial outfit has its uses, but it won't get me near the king himself. And that box of clothes I swiped was all butler garb…"

It was his fault the cadets were forced to dress as maids.

The sticky-fingered thief slipped into an empty classroom…

"…Hmm?"

…and found a male military uniform, neatly folded in the corner.

"Why a single uniform…? Welp, it's my size, so no looking a gift horse in the mouth."

He quickly started to change.

"Stroke of luck finding one small enough for... Hmm, weird armband. Head of the first-years? Better take that off. Then use my bangs to hide my face..."

He combed his hair down over his eyes, checking himself in the windowpane.

"This oughtta make it possible to be in a room with the king. Man, are they *still* clapping? What in the heck went down? No matter. I've got other fish to fry..."

And with that, Zalko left the classroom, headed for the king's chambers.

In said chambers, the king was excitedly observing the finishing touches of the festival preparations.

"Ho-ho-ho! Glad to see the young working so hard!"

He looked down at the pamphlet he'd personally put together.

"This romantic event...was well worth the effort it took to convince Profen. Now Maria will find true happiness. Right, Chrome?"

He beamed at his guard.

Chrome, however, was listening to a report from an underling, his square jaw set and extra grim.

"What? But...how can that be? If the king hears...I guess that's for the best. Does anyone else...?! Oof, that could be a problem."

The king smelled trouble, and his smile faded. "Chrome, did something happen?"

"Y-Your Majesty!" Chrome stammered. "N-no, nothing at all. Just a bit of trouble, won't take long."

"Oh? What kind of trouble?"

"Nothing you need to be concerned about. You relax and enjoy the festival, Your Majesty."

The king had faith in his guard and let the matter drop.

"If you insist. I'll focus on my own tasks. Shouldn't the statue be up on that pedestal by now?"

"Gah... W-well, it's the star of the show, so...we don't want to bring it out *too* early, do we?"

"Ah! Good point, Chrome. You've got the soul of an entertainer."

"Welp, I'd better go handle this."

Chrome grabbed a few other men and left the chambers.

Alone now, the king looked somewhat left out. He gazed out the window, feeling rather melancholy.

"If Chrome says there's no problem, I'm sure there isn't one. I'd better get dressed. Anyone there?"

At his call, a soldier appeared. "Yes, Sire?"

"Can you fetch my robe—mmph?!"

In a flash, the soldier had a handkerchief over the king's mouth. The king struggled valiantly but was soon rendered unconscious.

As he crumpled to the floor, the soldier—Zalko—tucked away the handkerchief, grinning.

"That went *very* well. Scarily so."

He placed a letter nearby, grabbed the king, and carried him onto the balcony.

Zalko secured a rope to the railing, checked the hold, and put the king over his shoulders, like he did this all the time.

"I did *not* see the king being left on his own like that... What happened to his security team?"

This had all been worryingly easy. And that was bugging him.

"There are good days and bad days, and I guess today was a good one? Either way, it's best I get outta here."

Talking like he was trying to convince himself, he rappelled down into the garden below, collected the rope, and was off like the wind.

Unaware of what was happening, the cadets were busy getting their maid café up and running.

"Put the prepared chicken and rice right here! Oh, and don't waste water! There's gonna be traffic at the well today."

Lloyd was barking orders, putting his cafeteria experience to good use. First- and second-years alike were following his lead without complaint.

"Absolutely, Sir Lloyd! I just love this adorably authoritative side of you! If you could just turn your eyes here?"

Selen was snapping pictures—no, wait, Riho and Phyllo were already stepping in.

"...Not the time."

"You have work to do."

Selen kept her eye to the viewfinder. She had a nightly news camera operator's sense of duty, fueled by her own passions.

"This *is* work, work that needs to be done, and done by me. Look at what he's wearing! It must be documented. And you'll both get copies, I promise."

"......Mm."

"Just don't take it too far."

Neither of them should ever go into politics. They were far too susceptible to bribes.

Then, Riho spotted Micona fussing with something to one side.

"Micona, whatcha doing?"

"Oh, Riho Flavin. Isn't it obvious? I'm creating a cool new dessert to pull the rug out from under Lloyd Belladonna."

She seemed well aware that he was beating her in the looks department, and she was trying to turn this into a cookery fight instead.

But she also knew that nobody could beat Lloyd in a conventional cook-off, so she was trying to find some other means.

Riho had no issues if it served the café well, so she grinned.

"Sounds great! Anything that boosts our sales is fine by me. Whatcha making?"

The glasses girl—now a glasses maid—stepped forward to explain.

"Soft serve," she said.

Riho looked again. They were using ice magic and kneading something with a spatula.

She made a face. This was disappointingly ordinary.

"That's it? It'll sell fine, but it's not exactly a 'cool new' dessert."

"That's where you're wrong!" Micona declared. "This is no ordinary ice cream. This is a local specialty soft serve."

"Meaning...?"

"Incorporating famous local products into soft serve is a tried-and-true tradition," glasses girl insisted. "No matter how uninspired the ingredient, once it's inside soft serve, it unleashes its true potential!"

"Well, it certainly makes an impression, I'll grant you. People do go for weird flavors." Then Riho frowned. "But what *is* Azami's thing? Can't say I've ever heard of any…"

Azami lay at the nexus of several trade routes and had a harbor—which meant it had the bounty of the sea and the farms, and little else to call its own.

Micona puffed her chest up even higher.

"But we do! The thing Azami is most famous for—skewers!"

"Uh…?!"

Paying no attention to Riho's look of horror, Micona and her cohorts held up a yellowish concoction, presumably the result of ground marinated meat mixed into cream.

"You're kidding…," Riho managed, visibly twitching, unable to tear her eyes from that lurid shade.

Since Azami had the best of both land and sea, there were many street stalls serving up kebabs with all manner of ingredients roasted on them. They *were* famous for it.

But it was something that could definitely only be eaten one way. To grind it up and put it in soft serve…? That sent a shiver down Riho's spine. These people were so focused on originality they'd forgotten that things had to *taste* good.

"One moment," Riho said. She grabbed a spoon, filled it with the soft serve, and headed in Phyllo's direction.

"……Mm?" Phyllo blinked at her.

"Sorry, Phyllo. Taste test this for me."

The spoon entered Phyllo's mouth.

There was a long silence.

"…That's gross. Whadda heck is it?"

Sheer revulsion had led to her developing an accent! Phyllo's usual deadpan was now screwed up into a horrifying rictus.

"Phyllo will eat anything, but not this…and it provoked a visible expression!"

At best, this might feed the pigs. Riho headed back to Micona.

"Okay, ladies and gents. Have you *tried* it?"

They were all smiles.

"Of course! It's a bit salty! The grease is all hardened and white. But it's a fascinatingly original flavor!"

"Yikes, they're too far gone."

Upon putting enough work into a dish, one might convince oneself into thinking it's actually good. They were showing all the symptoms, which left Riho clutching her head.

"We've got a product we can't move…"

Micona would normally be the one who stopped this stuff, but since she was leading the effort, there was no salvaging it.

"Fine, it's not like it'll be a *real* problem… Mm?"

At this point a real problem appeared, with a thunderous clatter.

Bam! Thud, thud, thud.

The doors had slammed open, and a group of soldiers marched in like they were occupying the place. The cadets all looked rattled.

But then they saw a familiar face.

"Colonel Chrome! And Colonel Choline? What's going on?"

"…And my sister."

Amid the crowd of soldiers were Chrome Molybdenum, Choline Sterase, and Mena Quinone.

And at the back of the group…

"Ugh, Rol?"

Rol Calcife. She'd been Riho's big sister figure at the orphanage they grew up in and had gone on to serve as headmaster at Rokujou Sorcery Academy before joining the Azami military.

She was looking around the room, projecting an air of confident power.

Meanwhile, Chrome just seemed astonished by all the maids.

"Why are you dressed like that?"

"Didn't anyone tell you?" Choline said. "The cadets are running a maid-and-butler café. I don't see any butlers… Did you not approve it?"

"I said we'd respect their initiative."

"They took that way too literally! Ha-ha!"

Chrome winced. It was definitely his job to stay on top of these things.

Meanwhile, Rol was muttering to herself. "They've got the tea, and the room...and plenty of cadets to help..."

At this point, Riho pounced. "Why are you here, Rol?! State your business!"

"...Oh, look at you. Is there money in it?"

"Of course! Why else?"

Riho was so quick to answer, Rol just started laughing.

"Glad you haven't changed," she said. "But we've got real trouble brewing. We're gonna need to take over the room."

"Huh? For what? Worth me sacrificing a guaranteed windfall?"

"...Many things are," Phyllo growled. Then she turned to Mena for an explanation. "...What's going on?"

"Phyllo! Ya see..."

But before she could answer, Rol cut her off. This was *her* deal.

"This'll be our investigation headquarters."

"Investigating what?" asked maid Lloyd.

Chrome turned to the room. "The statue's been stolen," he said.

"Statue... The one from Profen?! Wait, Rol!"

Rol was already starting to tear down the decorations.

"Know any other important statues? Security, you're over there. We'll get tea going. Mena!"

"On it! Tea for everyone!" Mena was already putting cups in soldiers' hands.

"Mena! Those are to sell!"

"Bill us for it later, Riho. And you know Rol's only here cause she trusts you and Lloyd."

"That's the thing, Riho," Choline chimed in, putting her hands together apologetically. "This can't get out. We gotta keep it to the staff on duty and as few other soldiers as we can."

Chrome bowed his head, asking all the cadets to help.

"You may be a bunch of nutbars, but you've got skills, and we need your help here."

"It's not just their heads I'm worried about! I mean...will ya *look* at Allan?"

"Mena! Don't kick a man when he's down!"

"Oh, I wouldn't dare touch you. I'd never sleep again! ...Ew, I'm serious. Don't touch your skirt like that—your little mannerisms are making me seriously ill..."

Mena's tone swiftly went from teasing to genuine disgust. She was covering her eyes to avoid seeing him.

"Aughhhh! Please don't sound so serious! I have a heart, you know!"

But despite Allan's shrieks, Rol was swiftly setting up shop. Puzzled by this, Selen tugged Choline's sleeve.

"So why is she being so intense?"

Choline sighed. "She thinks she can use this to bump herself up a rank."

Phyllo gave her former boss a half-lidded stare. "...Exactly how she did things at Rokujou Sorcery Academy."

"Okay, silence! Take your seats. Maids, you too. Prep can wait. Official orders."

Once everyone was seated, Rol nodded and wrote "Top Secret Investigation HQ" on the board. Everyone wondered if it was actually a good idea to write "secret" where everyone could see, but no one dared say that aloud.

The mood had suddenly grown urgent—because a group of high-ranking, heavily decorated soldiers had taken seats next to Rol. And they looked very concerned.

Lloyd wasn't familiar with the top brass, so he whispered, "Um, Allan, who are they?"

"From the left, the person in charge of intelligence and public relations, the one running security forces, and the top diplomatic liaison."

Those all sounded *very* important. This was like the briefing on a major crime, and everyone started to sweat it.

Deciding the time was right, Rol launched into a rundown of the facts.

"Before dawn this morning, someone stole the Statue of Love, on loan from Profen."

A stir ran through the room.

Rol feigned clearing her throat to quiet them down.

"From a diplomatic and security perspective, and to avoid turning the festival into chaos, we'd like to handle this incident internally. Only a select few soldiers are aware the theft occurred, and there's a gag order in place—if you let this leak, assume you have no future in the army."

As she rattled through her speech, Rol kept glancing at the top brass next to her. Their titles and medals were more than enough to turn the screws on all the untested cadets.

"So she's trying to make an impression on the top brass, working us to the bone, since she knows we can't argue."

"......She's so good at that."

"Yeah...we might have another year, but the upperclassmen are on the verge of placement. They can't argue with anything."

But even as they whispered, Rol wrapped things up.

"We're counting on your assistance. Moving on to the scene at the time of discovery..."

She pointed to a soldier, who saluted and took the floor.

"Near dawn, security forces arrived for their regular check of the treasure room interior and discovered that the Statue of Love—officially titled the Akizuki Statue—was no longer present. There were no signs of anything else missing, so we believe the statue was the thief's sole target."

"Approximately four hours passed between the evening and morning rounds. Were any suspicious figures spotted during that time?"

"We've checked with those on duty and all records kept, but found no such reports."

The top diplomat glanced at the top security guy, muttering, "We're sure this wasn't caused by your lax security, then? If this strains relations with Profen, it'll be my team left running frantically all over creation. Just thinking about that makes me..."

And if that was his *diplomatic* take...

The security head remained resolute. "Hardly words befitting a man who thoughtlessly brought in a valuable statue on the day before the festival and dumped all safety arrangements on us without any warning."

"Oh, so this is *my* fault?"

"This could very well be seen as an inside job your staff concocted to take my team down a peg."

The diplomat shot to his feet, clearly rattled by this charge. "H-how dare you make such an accusation!"

"If no suspicious figures were sighted, then an inside job is on the table. Rol, ensure we keep that possibility in mind during the investigation," the chief of intelligence and public relations said, interrupting the ugly political slugfest. He seemed committed to a proper military bearing—clearly a dedicated professional. But then he added, "If the statue's gone, the pamphlet is false advertising! If it gets out that the army has lost Profen's statue, our reputation will be in tatters! All our PR work will be flushed down the drain! And I'll make sure you two take the blame!"

""Is this really the time?!""

"Otherwise, it'll be my head on the chopping block…"

With politics and blame-shifting involved, this was no longer a simple robbery.

"We're not here to pass the buck. If we don't find the statue, assume all three of you are getting demoted."

"R-Rol!"

"W-we can't let that happen…"

"You must do something!"

They were now squealing like baby birds, and Rol gave them a very Buddha-esque smile.

"Never fear. That's why I'm here. I *will* find the statue."

"G-good."

"If you handle this matter, we'll remember your name."

"Ensure that you do."

They looked mollified—like children who've been scolded but hear kind words afterward.

Chrome had to doff his hat to it. "When you're that good at manipulating people, it's no surprise you rise to the top."

"She always was a master at it, yeah. Frustrating, but it helps at a time like this."

"Rol's motto is 'other people's problems are my chance to shine.' She's the queen of self-promotion."

Rol, meanwhile, had turned back to the cadets, glaring at them.

"You listening, cadets? You want to make an impression on us, work yourselves to the bone."

"Geez, never leaves an advantage unplowed."

"...You're a lot alike."

The PR guy didn't seem to trust the cadets. Despite his panic, he rose to admonish them once more.

"This absolutely *cannot* get out! Make *no* careless moves!"

At this point, Chrome rose to his feet, defending them.

"Rest assured, my students have the skills and experience to become immediate assets to any division."

"It ain't their skills but their character we're worried about! Several of them are prone to getting carried away," Choline muttered.

Chrome glared at her. Pot calling the kettle black.

"'Assets,' are they? Golly." Mena chuckled.

"There you have it," Rol said, and the three bigwigs settled down. "While you're up, Chrome, how's the king doing?"

"I managed to keep the statue's disappearance from him, so he should be enjoying the event..."

But even as he spoke—

"C-Colonel Chrome!"

—the door slammed open, and a guard came running in.

"What's this?"

"You found the statue?"

"Not judging from the look on his face..."

"Settle down. What is this?" Chrome asked.

The guard was gasping for breath, and Chrome had to give him a pat on the back.

He held up a letter.

"W-we found this!"

Chrome began to read. Choline, Mena, Rol, and the top brass all peered over his shoulders.

""""Wh-what the...?!"""""

Unsure what the letter said, the cadets could only stare.

"Um, excuse me?" Lloyd said, raising a hand. "What does it say?"

Chrome recovered his composure and read the letter aloud.

"'I have claimed your greatest treasure. To ensure its return, meet the following demands by the time the festival parade ends—'"

A stir ran through the room.

Phyllo raised her hand. "...And the demands?"

"'Dismiss Allan Toin Lidocaine and publicly announce that his feats were but lies.'"

"M-me?!" Maid skirts swirling, Allan leaped to his feet. He had no clue why he was involved.

Chrome kept reading. "'If you fail to meet these demands, you will never see the hostage again. From Zalko the Thief.'"

Zalko. That name brought a gasp from the room.

"*The* Zalko? The infamous thief, who'll steal anything you hire him to?!"

"So he stole the statue to undermine Allan's family... What a villain." Everyone was saying the same things.

Riho was trying not to grin. She folded her arms behind her head, glancing at Allan.

"I see!" she said. "Someone got jealous of you and hired a thief to handle it! Getting the great Zalko on you is a *real* feat."

"Hold up! They'd steal Profen's statue just to get at me?! Making enemies not just of Azami, but of Profen?!"

Mena rubbed her brow. "Yeah," she muttered. "That's the *point*. Take a scale—on one end, the fate of a single cadet, on the other, international relations. And this dude definitely wants to show off. Such a shame, Allan! You're about to be unemployed."

"Menaaaa! Can we at least *consider* rejecting the demands?"

"Exactly! Allan is Azami's ace! Our strongest warrior! His downfall would be a blow to our might! To people's faith in the army! Without Allan's incredible skills—"

"Lloyd, that's nice of you, but I'm really *not* as good as the stories say."

Allan was on the verge of tears. Lloyd's defense was adding a whole new layer of stress to the situation.

Meanwhile, Riho and Selen were in full-on tease mode.

©Nao Watanuki

"Calling a statue a hostage! I like it! As a reward, we definitely oughtta fire Allan."

"Payback for taking credit for something that wasn't yours. A long time coming, if you ask me! Just allow yourself to be fired so we can recover this statue."

"This is my life we're talking about here? Right…? Wait…"

The room was definitely leaning toward firing him, but then the PR honcho spoke up.

"Wait! As the man in charge of public relations, I must speak here. We cannot afford to eliminate Allan. He's the Dragon Slayer! The future hope of Azami! We may have exaggerated the stories *slightly*, early on, but he's followed through at every turn and been a splendid billboard. And you want to waste all those advertising funds?!"

"Now, now," the diplomat said, smiling ear to ear. "The sacrifice of this one man will recover the statue and salvage our relations with Profen."

"So my position doesn't matter to you at all?!"

The security soldier joined the mollification effort. "The loss of a treasure on loan from abroad is simply the bigger concern. It puts us in a tough spot."

"Where diplomacy can alleviate your concerns, I'll be happy to help. But the statue *must* be our top priority."

The cadets could only watch the top brass reveal their true colors.

If it meant the statue came back, what did Allan's life matter? Only Lloyd had the courage to argue otherwise.

"Y-you can't! I'm sure Allan has the strength to survive even if he leaves the army. He'll remain in high demand! But you can't just give in! I'm against it!"

"L-Lloyd…"

"And I really don't think the army should just be giving in to the demands of criminals."

Lloyd's honest opinion hit the three leaders and Rol like a ton of bricks.

"This is a highly delicate political matter, and no mere cadet—"

"Hmph, I hate to admit it, but he has a point." Micona—of all people— had his back.

"Micona!"

"As a soldier myself, I don't like seeing the Azami army played for fools. Let's find this statue, arrest the thief, and finish out the festival in style."

"That's what I'm saying!" wailed the PR guy. "You should all value your comrades! If Allan gets fired and we have to admit the stories were lies—I'm the one who insisted we tell everyone that he was our biggest hope! It'd be the end of me! A complete waste of advertising funds!"

How quickly that degenerated into truth.

"Hmm…what's your name, boy?" the security head said, glaring at Lloyd.

"Lloyd Belladonna, sir," Lloyd responded, not the least bit daunted. "I may not be dressed for it, but I am head of the first-years."

"…I'll remember you."

Rol clapped her hands, trying to regroup. "Fair enough. Recovering the statue from Zalko would certainly wrap things up neatly. Anyone got information on him?"

"I've got his dossier here," Chrome said, handing her a sheaf of papers. "I've printed copies for everyone, but let me know if there aren't enough. And this here's a list of locations in the Central District, where he might be lying low, and places where you might be able to hide a statue. Make good use of 'em."

"Huh…that's extra prepared of you, Chrome. Why did you have these?"

"Not important. Also ignore the 'Find Who's Hiding' part at the top."

"I'm even more lost…but fine."

Chrome proceeded to give everyone a brief rundown on the infamous thief.

"Good work," Rol said. "Since the statue's return is on the table, it'll be kept inside the kingdom, not too far from the castle itself. And the thief himself is likely lurking somewhere he can scope out the parade. Cadets, keep your eyes peeled."

"Rol!" Riho objected. "We've got a shop to run! We've got merchandise laid in and food prepped! We can't cancel now!"

The maid outfit did not match the greed underlying this protest.

"That's your problem to solve," Rol said dismissively.

"We're already short-staffed, and you want to siphon even more of us away? Customer service is everything at a maid café!"

The butler thing was long since forgotten.

Rol just rolled her eyes and turned to the security head. "The Zalko data and 'wanted' poster...the one with the reward on it."

"Hmm."

Rol took the page from him and put her arm over Riho's shoulder, showing her the document. "How's this hold up against your café's potential profits?"

"Er...you're kidding? He's worth that much?"

"You piss off the rich and famous, your price goes up. Worth dispatching a portion of your café crew, right?"

"Absolutely."

"Excellent."

Riho was already at the front of the hall—where Rol had been—speaking to all the cadets.

"Okay, kiddos! Time to show this sneak thief what military cadets can really do. For Azami! For our comrade, Allan! Let's catch this asshole!"

Allan looked up, saw the gold coins in her eyes, and made a face.

"...You're *so* transparent."

"Riho's having another episode. She always does, when money's involved. *Sigh.* Now we've got so much on our plate I won't be able to take Sir Lloyd to that romantic event."

"Selen, didn't you hear?" Choline said. "That event's been canceled."

"Why?"

"Because this statue was the centerpiece of it."

"It *was*?!"

"Profen people believe it's got matchmaking powers, so..."

The full facts on this sculpture got Selen motivated for very different reasons.

"Zalko must die! Nobody ruins romance on my watch! Crucify this thief!"

Clearly, she'd been planning on dragging Lloyd to the event, regardless of his desires, indulging her every fantasy, and somehow *scoring*. She probably had multiple marriage applications awaiting his signature hidden somewhere on her person.

Phyllo, meanwhile, was quietly smoldering. This did not show on her face, just in the heat haze behind her.

"...Selen, a proposition. Whoever of us takes out Zalko first...gets the right to attend the romance event."

Selen was rather taken aback, but she soon grinned.

"You're on, Phyllo. The two of us need to settle things once and for all."

Their eyes met. Tensions rose.

"Lloyd's in as much trouble as I am," Allan muttered.

But Lloyd was as oblivious to matters of the heart as he was to his own powers.

"Oh?" he said. "How so? I think you definitely have it worse."

"True...I really don't want to be discharged."

His attempt at sympathy had quickly been turned into a pity party.

As if fueled by all this emotion, Micona was ready for action.

"Second-years! We can't let our juniors hog all the glory. Time to show off our talents and get ourselves prime placements! And once we find the statue, Marie and I... Mwa-ha-ha."

Marie was never far from her mind. Unfortunately.

But despite her concluding mutter, the first half—particularly the bit about placements—definitely resonated. Everyone was getting gung ho.

"I know where I want to wind up!"

"Anywhere not provincial!"

"A desk job! Any desk job!"

Job-seeking students in any world will do anything to give themselves an advantage.

And hearing these myriad motivations was definitely making Chrome cringe.

"They're uh...reliable...," he managed.

"You can say that again, Chrome!" Mena chuckled.

Choline turned to the soldier who'd brought the letter. "So how'd the king take it?" she asked. "He didn't see this letter, right?"

"The king wasn't there."

"Cool! I bet he's so excited about the romantic event that he's gone to encourage the people setting it up or something."

No one suspected that a kidnapping and a theft had occurred simultaneously.

And since the letter itself had failed to be specific…

"Let's get this statue back from that scummy thief!"

"""""Yeahhhhhh!"""""

Without a single soul realizing that Zalko was holding the king hostage, everyone was hell-bent on recovering the statue. This confusion would not get cleared up anytime soon. God bless.

As for the king himself, he was in a dimly lit room, bound, and sprawled upon the floor.

A whiff of mold was in the air, a faint glow hovered around the curtains, and distant sounds of the festival preparations could be heard. There was a box of clothes hidden at the back of the room—the purloined butler garb.

Between being gagged and being unable to move his arms and legs, the king realized what fate had befallen him, but did not panic. He calmly met his captor's gaze.

"Sorry, hardly the place to bring a king," Zalko said, superficially polite. He was still wearing the stolen military uniform and bobbed his head once.

"…………"

Seeing the king disinclined to kick up a fuss, or perhaps just seeing a part of his personality—Zalko loosened the king's gag.

"No use yelling for help. I made sure to pick a spot out of earshot."

"What are you trying to accomplish?"

Zalko clapped his hands, impressed with the king's aplomb.

"This is a monarch with guts! I wish my haughty employer would take a few tips from you."

"Is your client…after my life?"

"No, no. I make it a rule never to take lives. My client has his goals, and I'm doing my part…and that's all I can really tell you."

Zalko's tone had the specific kind of conceit that proved he considered his work an *art*.

But the king stuck to his guns.

"I'll warn you not to underestimate the Azami army. They'll soon find me."

"We'll see. Even if they do, I can handle myself—and I won't go down easy."

"I suppose we'll find out." The king closed his eyes, as if he had no doubt rescue was already on its way. Zalko was clearly relishing the challenge.

"They will come," said the king. "They're my steadfast companions! We're all one big family!"

As for the subordinates he had such complete faith in...

"So we can't have the king finding out about this! If you see him, you *know nothing*!"

"Yes, sir!"

"If he speaks to you, ignore him!"

"Yes, sir!"

"He's off god-knows-where, riling people up about his event, so take care! He could be anywhere!"

"Yes, sir!"

"All right! Find that statue! Move, maggots!"

"Yes, sir!"

If the king heard that, he'd likely sob himself to sleep. Some "family"! Rol's brutal orders sent the soldiers racing to their positions.

The three bigwigs and a few of their subordinates remained, occupying the kitchen-waiting room-statue search headquarters. Fidgeting soldiers...students in maid uniforms...it was awkward for everyone.

Riho was already way past caring about her clothes. She had her work rosters out on a table. They had columns for dining floor, kitchen, security, and free time, and she added a new one for statue searching.

"Um, so canceling all free time and most security work and putting that all toward statue duty... Don't need many here... Argh, fine, I'll let a few boy maids work the floor. Sacrifices must be made! Why aren't those butler uniforms here?"

Grumbling away, she never stopped her red pen from moving. Soon she had the whole roster fixed, so swiftly it earned her a cheer.

"I'll give you this one, Riho Flavin."

"Heh-heh-heh. Well, even I wanna do what's right sometimes."

Everyone decided against adding, "When there's money in it."

While a bit short-staffed, the maid café itself was fully operational, and those on security shifts were tasked with double duty.

"Make sure the citizens are enjoying the festival while searching for the statue, patrolling to ensure no other trouble happens—lots to do. All for Allan! All for Azami. All so we can be the soldiers we've always dreamed of being."

""""Yeah!"""""

Lloyd's speech was very enthusiastic, and his skirts fluttered a lot. It got everyone fired up.

The security head was watching closely.

"You wouldn't know it to look at him...but that kid's got mettle. Been a long time since anyone had the balls to stand up to me."

"Lloyd Belladonna, you mean?" said the top diplomat, perking up his ears.

"The way he looks...it's the polar opposite of a soldier. That might actually work wonders for PR! He'd look good on a poster."

The PR man had a very different take, but the other two just ignored him, leaning in close—as if they'd forgotten their earlier squabble.

"Looking at him takes me way back," the security head said. "Back then, I let my heart drive me, too."

"Yeah, we all did, once. But our jobs demand compromise. Calculated stances."

The diplomat flicked the medals on his chest derisively. They jingled like a baby's toys.

"I never imagined I'd have this much riding on my shoulders. Sometimes I'm not sure if I'm protecting the country or my own position as security chief. Ever feel that way?"

"Well, well. I suspect we all do." The diplomat chuckled. Knowing the feeling only too well.

The security honcho rose to his feet and headed for the door.

"Oh, what now?"

"Got to thinking how I used to do things. Thought I'd ask a few questions."

"That boy got you motivated? Ha-ha."

The diplomat got up himself.

"You too?"

"Well, if you get results, that leaves us looking inept! That means I've got to put in some legwork myself."

They laughed at each other and headed out.

Rol blinked after them.

"If those two make a move...Lloyd's far more influential than I suspected."

She looked at Phyllo and her newfound (if still subtle) expressions. She looked at Riho, clearly relishing life once more.

"Rol," called out the PR man, "Can I have some tea? Oh, what's that yellow soft serve? Caramel?"

This man appeared entirely unmoved by anything happening around him, but Rol elected to leave that unmentioned.

"His potential is immeasurable. Allan's got a tall task, riding his coattails. Still..." Rol narrowed her eyes, seeing Lloyd and Riho chattering away. "If he's as strong of spirit as he is in battle...can't believe I was so wrong. Wish he were working for me."

The PR man took a bite of the kebab-flavored soft serve and let out a strangled moan, which Rol pointedly ignored.

Everyone working here had different motives—and the festival itself was about to begin.

Chapter 2

A Bemused Flopsweat: Suppose a Boss Realized His Staff Were BFFs with the Client's CEO and CCO at the Sales Pitch

Pop! Pop! Pop!

Little red and yellow fireworks shot upward toward the blue skies.

At this signal, the international flag-festooned gate opened, and the crowd flooded in, locals and out-of-town visitors alike. Some of them were so eager they broke into a run.

People argued about whether to score a good spot to watch the parade or pick up a drink and some kebabs first—the sounds of peace. Costumed staff handed out balloons, to the delight of children.

The guards near the gates were checking every face, eyes extra vigilant.

Soldiers searching for Zalko were frantic amid the excited crowd—and the chaos of the carnival was just getting started.

Rol was at the head of the search headquarters, receiving reports.

"Front gate, all clear."

"Roger, stay alert."

"Service entrance. No statues, no suspicious peeps."

"Roger, make sure you check everything."

"Table one, two omelets with ketchup hearts."

"Roger, table…huh?"

"Table two wants to play rock-paper-scissors."

"…………"

"Yo, Rol! Don't just sit there! Help get these omelets on!"

Riho was busy cooking up a storm—in full maid garb. There was sweat on her brow.

The statue mattered, but if they canceled the café, people might get suspicious—and the moment it opened, it was jam-packed. Even as the statue search soldiers reported in, cadets in maid clothes were running back and forth.

"Riho, I'm already working!"

"And we're swamped! I put several kitchen staff on your search detail. You can warm up the chicken and rice while you listen to the reports!"

"What kind of supervisor does dual duty as—?"

Pop-pop-pop!

"Mm? Sorry, can't hear you over all this frying; you'll have to talk louder!"

"If I can't even hear the reports, I really can't help!" Rol yelled.

Riho was making short work of her order.

"Omelets up! Put the hearts on 'em."

"On it!" a deep voice boomed. The second-year cadet furrowed his brow, grimly drawing hearts in ketchup. If this frenzy were to be seen, customers would start squawking about deception and lawsuits.

"Did *not* see us hitting peak rush the moment the place opened," Riho grumbled. "But the real miscalculation…"

She glanced out at the main floor, where—

"Lloyd! Over here!"

"Lloyd-i-poo!"

"Lloyd! Hah! Hah!"

"Coming! Just one moment!"

Most of the crowd were here for Lloyd and Lloyd alone.

While he was mobbed by patrons of every gender, Micona was working alongside him…and getting far less attention, to her annoyance.

"Dammit, I subject myself to this humiliation…and I'm a girl! How is Lloyd Belladonna's maid look winning over mine?!"

"Micona, rock-paper-scissors!"

"*What?!* You want a fist to the *face?*"

"O-oh-ho?!" (A squeal, overjoyed.)

A subset of their customer base *really* seemed to dig her style.

Between the two of them, they were keeping the place hopping.

Riho pointed Rol toward the bustle, explaining, "He was supposed to be our kitchen linchpin but is, like, five times as popular as we thought, so…we need help, bad."

"What do you think the priority is here? The statue or your maid café management?"

"They're both important, Rol. If we gotta close up, and people ask questions, that's a problem for you. And crowds bring in information."

Just like how video games always make you go to bars to ask questions, this place was less a bar than a den of iniquity.

As they spoke, maid Allan returned from the floor.

"I asked around, merc. Everyone laughed. It was mortifying."

"Hang in there, Allan."

"My career's on the line, so yeah. Micona's gathering info between RPS bouts."

"One, two—PAPER!"

Craaack! (That's the sound of the thunderous clap of her palm against a man's cheek.)

"Eek! Thank you very much!"

"If you're grateful, tell me everything you know! See any thieves around?"

"Does that technically count as rock-paper-scissors?"

"Allan… As long as the customers as satisfied…"

Rol had plenty of questions, but the cadets were doing their part to further the investigation, so she couldn't complain.

"Geez…well, I'm not frying anything. Can't be drowning out the reports."

"Can you actually cook?"

"Who was it kept you fed when you only had one arm functioning?"

"Riiight. That was a long time ago."

Misty-eyed from reminiscing, Rol started peeling fruit.

For a moment, they really looked like sisters. "Money or promotions, they're both always hungry, it seems," Allan muttered.

"'Scuse me! Omelet and fruit platter!"

""On it!""

Lloyd was looking tired, and he blinked when Rol and Riho answered as one.

Some time later, in the building across from their classroom...
On the roof below the clear skies, a young man's hair was tousled by the wind.
"What a breeze! A beautiful day for filming."
Shouma. He had found a pamphlet with Lloyd's café listed in it and had made a beeline for a roof with a view, on standby.
"I know Lloyd's café is in there. From here, I can get some good footage of him working."
"If I may ask one thing, Shouma," the older man next to him said.
"Sure thing, Sou!"
"What manner of establishment is a maid-and-butler café?"
Shouma's grin broadened. "Like a fetish shop for people who can't afford servants?" he said, possibly a bit too on the nose. You've got to sell the dreams, man. That menu wasn't cheap.
"Yet, doesn't even sell drinks? For Lloyd to be working there is... hardly heroic."
"Don't worry! He'll be in the kitchen. He's a great cook! Or maybe waiting tables as a butler? I can see him taking orders like a boss."
"Personally, I'd say an apron over his army uniform would be effective enough."
"Oh, also passionate! You didn't save the world for nothing, Sou!"
Passionate how? ...Never mind.
"Spare me," Sou said, not batting an eye. "All I wish is to have Lloyd wrest the hero's title from me so that I can fade from this mortal coil."
"True that... Oh, they're open!"
Shouma got his camera on the tripod and peered through the viewfinder.
And—
"............"
There was a long silence.
"What's wrong, Shouma?"
"............" *Tug, tug.*

Without a word, Shouma urged Sou to take a look for himself. A rare break in the machine-gun fire of his verbiage—and his nose was bleeding. Baffled, Sou leaned in.

And—

"......................"

Sou, likewise, froze to the spot, unable to speak.

Then he slowly pulled himself away from the viewfinder, turning to face Shouma.

"Shouma, remind me of our purpose here."

"Sou, we're here to get footage of Lloyd at the festival, loved by everyone. As part of a narrative, we'll leave it for future generations, showing how his heroism saved the world."

"Yes. All so they may understand how great he truly was."

""But…""

Their voices overlapped. They leaned over the railing, peering into Lloyd's classroom.

And what their eyes beheld—was Lloyd in his maid uniform.

""He's a bit *too* cute!""

Perfect harmony. Cheeks rosy red.

"We can't! We can't even make this into a scene where 'the hero has his silly side'! It's too memorable! Everything that actually matters will be instantly forgotten! The boy's heroic adventure will become the cross-dresser's road to fame and fortune!"

"It'll go off the rails. Worst case scenario, people will think, 'I knew it! Sou was the *real* hero all along!' and I'll *boost* my own notoriety! The opposite of what I want! The opposite!"

"Impossible. We can never let this footage go public. This is for our eyes only."

Shouma peered through the lens again, muttering about light levels, adjusting focus.

"Shouma…ensure I get a copy."

They both loooooved Lloyd.

But the shockingly flawless maid look was far too removed from their heroic ideal. "That's not the kind of love I wanted to capture!" Shouma wailed.

"Wipe your nosebleed," Sou said, offering a handkerchief.

"I mean, Sou…it's too much! What happened to the butlers?!"

He shoved the handkerchief up his nostrils, stopping the bleeding. It left his voice a bit muffled.

"We can't give up yet," Sou said. "Certainly, this footage is for our use only, but he's a soldier! He'll have patrol duties later."

"Right! True enough. That should let us get some footage of him being beloved in a more typical sense."

He yanked the handkerchief out of his nose with an audible *pop.*

"You remain here, filming every second of maid Lloyd. I'll review the footage at my leisure later on."

"You got it, Sou! It'll be real passionate! Mm? But where are you going?"

"I thought I spied a used bookstore."

"Books? Passionate! We'll meet up later, then."

Sou nodded, and headed across the square—clearly, his business at the bookstore was urgent.

Meanwhile, what was happening with the kidnapped king?

He was in a darkened storeroom, his eyes closed, calmly waiting for rescue.

Wasting energy screaming or struggling would just leave him too tired to move when the time came. A wise choice.

And what allowed him to remain calm despite the peril? In a word—faith.

Four years had passed between Abaddon's possessing him and his release. His former guard, Chrome, and his daughter, Maria, had never once given up, leaving no stone unturned in their quest to rescue him.

When Jiou attacked, his subordinates and those cadets had really come through.

His utter faith in them allowed him to keep his wits about him, even with his life on the line.

"You're a great man. Not even kidding. That's a quality a monarch *needs.*"

Zalko seemed to be craving shocked looks or at least...*any* reaction. He couldn't keep himself from prodding the man.

Between the letter left behind and his reluctance to give his client updates—you could call him an "entertainer," but maybe he was just an attention whore.

The king remained stonily silent.

Zalko just kept yammering.

"I've been infiltrating the military academy and the Central District for a month now...and found the perfect place to stow a kidnappee. What luck, I thought!"

"............"

"This storeroom's clearly been abandoned for years. Good distance from the campus square, hidden by trees nobody's pruned—almost nobody knows the building even exists."

For the first time, the king responded, speaking quietly.

"But I have faith. My guards and the cadets will find me here."

Zalko appeared delighted by this show of confidence—

Click! Rattle, rattle.

The door unlocked and slid open.

There stood a blond girl with bloodshot eyes.

Mere seconds after insisting they could not be found, a soldier was here. Zalko could not disguise his shock, and he leaped to his feet.

"Wh-who are you?!"

The king's face lit up, certain someone was here to rescue him. He peered through the sunlight streaming in.

"Oh! You're—"

Her cursed belt wriggling, Selen swept in. Eyes like daggers, sweat upon her brow—she'd clearly run all the way here.

"Colonel Chrome's information was right. This would be a perfect place to hide something."

She glanced down at the list in her hand.

"But there's no sign of the object we seek, Mistress," Vritra said, the buckle scanning the room. "Mm?"

"What is it, Vritra...? Oh."

Both of them spotted the king, bound and sprawled upon the floor.

Their eyes met. The king smiled.

He'd been waiting—keeping faith in his heart, despite his fears. He called her name.

"Selen, was it? The cadet they call the Cursed Belt Princess—?"

Just as he was about to yell, "Come, save me! I am the king you seek!"…

"I must be hearing things," Selen said, averting her eyes.

"Wh-whaaaat?!"

The king's jaw dropped so hard the noise echoed. Their eyes had met! And she pretended not to see him! Even though he was *clearly* kidnapped!

It was like being accosted by muggers and seeing a beat cop stroll right on by.

But Selen's sole goal was locating the Statue of Love. She had no idea the king had been kidnapped, so perhaps you could argue she had some excuse.

And she'd been specifically instructed to ignore the king entirely, lest she accidentally let the statue's disappearance slip.

She and Vritra were furiously whispering.

"No signs of the statue."

"Then we had better leave before the king finds out about the disappearance, Mistress."

"Indeed. I don't recognize that soldier with him… What are they up to?"

"Probably practicing an escape act for this event of his."

"That explains it. No one would ever tie up a king otherwise! Let's get going."

And with that, they were gone. Zalko had pulled out a knife to eliminate them but was left uselessly holding it, a dazed look on his face.

The king had been certain his salvation was at hand and could not believe anyone would simply ignore him—so he was equally dazed. There was a long silence, and then they looked at each other. Both of their heads tilted to one side.

©Nao Watanuki

"Um, what? Did I mess that up?" the king asked.

"That's what I wanna know, Your Majesty. Can't believe anyone found us, but even more amazed she just went away without doing *anything*."

For a moment, they both considered the matter.

"Oh! She went to get backup. She knew she couldn't handle this herself!"

"Aha! That makes more sense. Must be true. But that's bad news for me! Mind if we change hideouts?"

"Oh, go right ahead. I have faith in my men and those cadets. They'll find me no matter where we are."

"Yet, you sure looked like an abandoned puppy there..."

Zalko moved to put the king to sleep again—

Rattle, rattle.

—when the door opened once more.

There stood a girl with no expression—Phyllo. She had the same "Find Who's Hiding" flyer in her hand. Chrome's scheme was working out well.

"......Mm."

She looked around the room, not batting an eye, but saw something resembling the object she sought and was on it in a flash.

"Oh! See! She brought in backup! Though it seems a bit fast for that..."

"Damn, I should have moved faster! Should I knock her out, too?"

"Phyllo! You're Mena Quinone's sister, the martial artist, yes? I'm over here!"

Phyllo turned toward the voice and—

"......Ugh."

She put in no effort to hide it. Poker faces were her whole thing, but those eyebrows had definitely moved marginally closer together.

"What *is* this? What did I do?!"

Certain the statue wasn't here, Phyllo tried to sneak away, following Rol's specific orders to ignore the king.

"...I saw nothing."

"That's a lie! Our eyes met! Don't ignore me! I'm the king! What's your problem?! Do you not see what's going on here?"

Phyllo took another look.

The king, tied up. A strange soldier bent over next to him.

Phyllo knew...this must be some sort of *role play*. The king was really going all out for this romantic event, revealing his own fetishes to the world.

"..........Have fun," she said. And she was gone.

"Have *fun*?! What could be fun about a tied-up king?!"

The look on Zalko's face suggested he was no longer sure he even had the right king. The king himself was simply bewildered.

Back to the booming butlerless maid café!

The soldiers-dressed-as-maids concept had created quite a stir, and the classroom had been at maximum capacity since the moment the festival gates opened.

Just before noon, they finally had a brief lull—and though they'd been open for a while now, not one person had pointed out the lack of butlers. One look at maid Lloyd and all such concerns vanished.

The line of customers waiting for Micona to belittle them was growing shorter, but not dying entirely, which was impressive...though concerning for the future of Azami.

While she was slapping another customer across the face, soldiers who'd been on free time or security shifts came tromping back in.

Each of them made their reports to Rol. Next to her, Riho was flat out on a desk.

"This late already? Ugh...my wrists hurt..."

She'd been shaking pans in the kitchen for *hours*.

Rol glanced up from her reports. "There's no point in you having a maid uniform on, Riho. But you still shouldn't leave your legs spread like that..."

"Nobody's looking up *my* skirts," Riho growled. "You get anywhere? Anyone spot Zalko or the statue?"

Rol shook her head, looking concerned. "Not a single clue. No reports of anyone suspicious, or even reports of reports. The average customer here is far more suspect."

"Don't remind me."

Maybe best left unsaid, yes.

"It's almost noon. We can't afford to rest. You've got to drag yourself away from the maid café and help with the search."

"Will do."

"I'm counting on you."

"......Got it."

Rol gave Riho a pat on her shoulders and started sticking notes with info and reports onto the blackboard. She might have just been gunning for a promotion, but she was working for it, and...that took Riho back.

Until Lloyd pressed a glass of cold water against her brow.

"Aaaah! Oh, Lloyd."

Startled out of her reverie, she turned to find Lloyd with an impish grin.

"You look worn out, Riho. Hovering over a fire can make you really thirsty, so I brought you some water."

"Thanks."

He sat down next to her. Clearly used to the skirts now, he naturally folded the fabric to avoid wrinkles. A total girl move, and it didn't even look out of place.

"I'm pretty worn out, too. The customers sure were in a tizzy!"

"For real. Definitely all your charm, Lloyd," Riho teased—payback for the cold glass.

He turned red, arguing. "I-it wasn't me! Everyone looks great. Allan was knocking 'em dead!"

"That's one word for it! Ha-ha-ha." Riho joked, "He could go to war dressed like that and emerge triumphant."

They could see slivers of his bulging muscles from under his skirt.

"Good thing I put Phyllo and Selen on security. If they'd seen men and women alike begging to have you wait on them they'd have lost it. You're winning by a mile, right?"

"Not really, no. Micona actually got far more requests."

"She's...working her angle."

They looked over at her.

＊　　＊　　＊

"Micona! Can we do rock-paper-scissors again? Paper on my butt, please."

"You really are a piece of shit. Don't come back."

"Thank you very much! It's been an honor!"

Azami's dark side was in action.

"I had no idea rock-paper-scissors had such terrifying rules in the city."

"Oh, that's an exception. Usually hitting people during it would be criminal."

Riho smoothly stepped in to clear up that confusion. An urgent move—if she made a rock and punched someone, there'd be nothing left of them.

Lloyd turned his attention to Riho's appearance.

"You should work some tables, Riho. I think you'd be pretty popular."

"Me? No way."

"I swear! You're cute. They'll love you."

"Ah!"

Lloyd was trying to share the suffering and evoke some sympathy, but it got to her the wrong way. Her reaction was definitely a "comedy sketch" level of exaggeration.

Rol and Allan and other cadets watching from the sidelines were all grinning at them.

"Nice blush, merc."

"You trying to hide under the table?"

"Quit teasing and get to work! Argh."

Riho hung her head—but did snap her legs together.

Lloyd clapped his hands. "I know," he said. "You've been working harder than anyone, making rosters, getting equipment—I should make it up to you."

"Huh? Why now?"

"An official thanks from the head of the first-years. And I'm dressed like this...so allow me to serve, milady."

"Uh...then..."

Tempted, Riho pondered what she should ask for. But as if sensing the mood, her friends arrived to interfere.

"Gosh, no idea why my belt just wound around you like that, Riho."

"......My hands just compulsively formed the iron claw."

"Aughhh! Hey! That hurts! Ow! Phyllo, your shit is seriously too much!"

"......You know why."

"Sheesh, I leave for one minute and look what happens!"

"Owwww... W-welcome back? Well? Find any clues?"

"No detail too small!"

"Um...well, the king was with some strange soldier practicing a secret trick for some event or other."

"...Was that what I saw? I assumed..."

"Assumed what?"

"......Mm."

Unable to admit, in front of a pure boy like Lloyd, that she'd thought two men were finding love in their declining years, she settled for a grunt.

"Well, glad to hear he's not involved in the statue thing. But a secret trick? Guess that'll be something to look forward to," Riho responded.

Lloyd shot to his feet, motivated. The skirts levitated a bit too high, but Selen's belt blocked it and nobody saw anything.

"Okay! Then I'll go look! If the king's that excited, we've gotta find it! Lemme just change first."

And he was gone.

Selen and Phyllo tried to go with him, but Riho snapped, "Don't you follow Lloyd into the changing room! You've got your own outfits to get on. You're working maid shifts next!"

"No!" Selen gasped, tears in her eyes. "I want to work *with* Sir Lloyd! I'll search harder than anyone!"

"I've got you scheduled for time together later. Settle down."

"...Mm, fine."

Just then, a yelp went up from the room in back—where Lloyd was changing.

"Wh-what's with Lloyd? Selen's right here!" Riho called out.

"Slander!"

Lloyd soon emerged, still in his maid outfit.

"Wh-what's wrong, Lloyd?"

"My uniform is missing! I found the armband, but...did anyone see the rest?"

"Selen, fork it over."

"Slander and defamation! I was so preoccupied with the statue, I completely forgot about it. Shame."

"......Riho, I think she's clean."

Selen looked so grief-stricken, everyone knew she *would* have done the crime if it had occurred to her.

"Well, probably someone just assumed it was forgotten or lost. I guess you'll have to work security dressed like that!"

"Erp?!"

"It'll be good advertising for us. And you look good! Just tell everyone about the maid café. You said you'd do something for me, right?"

She was going to get payback for his teasing her. Lloyd turned red but was forced to agree.

"But...if not Selen...then Alka?" Riho said.

Selen jumped at that. "If nobody saw it happen, she's a likely candidate...but at the cost of blowing a once-in-a-lifetime chance to drool over maid Lloyd?"

"......You've convinced me."

Alka was still the prime suspect, though. Where could she be? Riho folded her arms like a veteran detective. This was convincing, even in maid clothes.

"And what happened to our butler uniforms? Did the delivery company blow it? And where *is* Alka? I figured she and Marie would be here by now."

As for the subjects of their suspicion...

"Why did you bring this to my house?! Throw it away!"

"I wish I could! I just can't! Too many memories! I can't just declutter it!"

Alka had brought the Statue of Love—her own creation—to Marie's shop.

Shortly after Lloyd had left to prep the maid café, Alka had appeared with a nine-foot-tall *thing*. Marie had sleepily stubbed her toe on it, looked up, and screamed—bothering the neighbors again.

Alka had tried to ditch it and had run, but had been caught, and they'd been arguing ever since.

"Why does it have to be *here*?! Drop that crap in Kunlun! And this is an exhibit for the Military Festival, right?"

"If I put it in Kunlun, the villagers will all get curious and ask too many questions, and if I say nothing, they'll decide it wards off evil or is some sort of weapon, and there's nothing more horrifying than hearing people's interpretations of your art!"

"You're not even making sense! Argh, I thought this romantic event might actually get me somewhere, but this lump of rock's so ugly that if I hauled it to a museum, they'd charge me a disposal fee!"

Unaware that this "art" was supposed to be displayed at that romantic event, Marie was cheerily trash-talking it. So much for its blessings. (It never had any.)

Alka was looking grumpier by the second, but Marie kept on the attack.

"They'll be in a panic by now! Give it back!"

"It's mortifying! I can't let it be displayed in public! I'll give it back after the festival…so keep it until then!"

"I can't have something this imposing in my shop! No one would ever come back!"

"No one ever comes here anyway. I'm gonna go hit up the festival! After I get my fieldwork done. You go on ahead!"

"No, wait! Kid grandma! No, owwww! My leg cramped!"

That rune curse was still in effect.

Marie rolled across the floor, hit her head on the statue, and groaned some more.

"Runes are far too strong now that I have my power back," Alka said, giving her a look of pity. "But this is my chance to skedaddle!"

She whipped out a crystal and vanished back to Kunlun, leaving Marie huddled on the floor, crying.

The bells of noon rang empty in her ears.

*　　*　　*

Dong...dong... The noon bells echoed.

And the festival was only getting busier.

Countless stalls lined the campus to the castle: The artillery division's cannon chocolate bananas. The audit department's crepes. The supply transportation team's extra-filling onigiri. Each military division was trying to match the theme of their work.

Crowds formed around the stalls, and moving through those crowds were soldiers on security duty, on the lookout for suspicious activity. Areas of the country ordinarily off limits were open today, which carried a risk that malcontents would try something. And with a statue already gone missing, their glares were extra gnarly.

Among their number was a member of the royal guard, Mena—eyes smiley, munching on a candy apple as she watched the crowds stream by.

"Looks like nobody's stupid enough to pick pockets on military grounds...except for this Zalko dude."

An elusive master of disguise, Zalko was someone whose face no one knew—they weren't even sure "he" was the right pronoun to use for the thief. He must have been lurking somewhere in the Central District so he could tell if they'd announced Allan's dismissal, but with no one having any information to go on, he'd be hard to find.

"All we can do is mark anyone who looks like they could be wearing a disguise... Sheesh, didn't think my acting experience would help me with something like this."

Mena had spent some time in showbiz, acting under the stage name "Mina." And that had given her a knack for spotting suspicious behaviors—seeing through disguises and performances. They were still talking about how she'd spotted the wig on a clerk who'd kept his baldness a secret for a decade.

"And Rokujou sent me another movie offer...starting over on that last one, since the mess prevented them from releasing it. I don't think so. I'll just call in sick."

Might as well just retire the whole actress thing, it seemed. She'd achieved her goals in that field; now she could focus on her military career.

Hiding her identity and getting stuck filming for days on end in another country was not worth the trouble.

Mena kept telling herself that, but something the boy had said stuck with her.

"I think you're marvelous, Mina."

Not realizing who she really was, he'd been effusively complimentary. And every time she remembered that, she felt a pang in her heart.

"……Hearing that from fans makes it hard to quit."

As she got lost in thought, a stir ran through the crowd around her. It wasn't exactly a panic, but there were definitely some shrill voices.

Concerned, Mena turned toward the cries. "What? Is someone famous…?"

She saw—Lloyd. Walking. Dressed…as a maid.

It looked *insanely* good, and everyone who saw him let out a cry, stopping in their tracks.

Surrounded, he looked baffled. Every few steps he took, someone asked him what this was for, and he dutifully explained that the military academy was putting on a maid café in one of the classrooms.

Then he saw a familiar face—Mena—and came over.

"Hi there, Mena!"

"L-Lloyd?!"

He pushed his way through the crowds, sweat plastering his bangs to his face. Getting this far had clearly been a grueling gauntlet.

Mena glanced at the crowd and shooed them away, "Don't be weird about it; we don't wanna have to correct anyone, do we?"

But why was he wandering around dressed like this?

"What's with the getup?! Do you just…*like* it? Some frontiers are best left unexplored!"

This was shaping up to be a real lecture. Her eyes were wide open! She was genuinely concerned about where his enthusiasms might lead him.

"Oh, no!" Lloyd said, blushing. "You see, my uniform disappeared. Only my armband was left behind."

"And you grilled Selen already?"

No pause for thought; Selen's accomplishments had earned her unwavering trust.

Lloyd laughed. "It's not her," he assured Mena. "They said I should advertise the shop while I worked security. Did you happen to see a box this big that said 'clothing' on it?"

He held his arms out, but Mena shook her head.

"Nothing like that, no. I'll tell you if I spot it! So what's the plan with that outfit?"

"I'm here to relieve your shift, Mena."

"Ah-ha-ha. The getup will be good advertising, but can you actually work security dressed in those clothes?"

She had a very good point.

"I figure it's like going undercover, or a decoy strategy? People act cautious when they see soldiers around. That's what I'm telling myself anyway."

A slight hint of discomfort there. It was his newfound "head of the first-years" duty that drove him to it.

"Riho sure knows how to sell anyone on anything. But you'll just be the cause of a whole different kind of crime…"

Seeing him look so innocent and cute had her all flustered. He was so cute that even girls like her were into it.

"What's wrong?"

"N-nothing. You just…look good in everything. I thought that back in Rokujou, too."

"Mm? Were you with us?"

He still hadn't worked out that Mina and Mena were the same person.

"Uh."

"Oh, you did show up later all dressed up? But why was that? I've been wondering."

Lloyd got persistent at the worst times. And the maid outfit made it very hard to focus.

A voice bellowed above the crowds.

"I! Am! In! Azamiiiii! Who is that? I thought! But it was MENA!"

"Quiet. You're so loud."

"Ubi! Harsh! No, wait—the festival is so filled with fiery passion you fear I'll get heatstroke, so you're cooling me off with your frosty tone! That's my wife-slash-bodyguard for you! My passions are *all yours*."

"Should I open an artery? You'll cool off in *seconds*."

The man was as boisterous as the girl was impassive—the king of Rokujou, Sardin Valyl-Tyrosine, and his wife, Ubi.

They seemed to be here incognito, so Sardin was wearing a T-shirt, plain pants, and sunglasses. And Mena—this king's actual daughter—was extremely rattled by her father's surprise appearance.

"D-Dad...," she whispered.

"Here I am!"

"You shouldn't be! You're king... Should you just be wandering around?"

"Have you forgotten? My wife—your mother—is an excellent bodyguard. That's what made me fall in love in the first place! I'm never safer than when I'm with my beloved Ubi."

Mena would gladly pay money to not hear how her parents met, but not only was she forced to listen to it, it was happening in public. Fury made her eyes bulge.

"Have you lost it? You came all the way here just to dote on her?"

"Ubi, my love...our daughter's being cruel."

"Natie, even if it's true, you're still liable for defamation, so careful."

"That was a roundabout agreement! I'm a king, not an emperor parading his new clothes!"

They were just doing a vaudeville act now, and Mena sighed dramatically.

"Why are you even *here*?"

"What else? Azami and Rokujou are allies, so I was formally invited! And there was no sign of the king of Azami, so my wife and I slipped out for a date! I heard there was a romantic event here, so I thought I'd tell her how much I love her—ow, my ribs!"

He'd been interrupted by a swift karate chop, possibly an attempt by Ubi to hide her blush, but probably not worth the risk of cracked ribs.

"There's no need for that."

"Darling..."

"I know how you feel. No need to put it in words."

"D-darling!"

Clutching his side, tears streaming beneath his sunglasses, Ubi ignored him, turning back to her daughter. "Sorry to surprise you. How's it going?"

"I'm getting on," Mena said, a mischievous glint in her eye. "Glad to see both of you unchanged. Enjoy that romantic event!"

"You aren't going to give it a try yourself?" Ubi said, turning the tables. She lowered her voice to a whisper. "Once you finish hanging out with you girlfriend here, you could take Lloyd there, tell him how you feel."

"Uh, wait..."

"Oh! I shouldn't say anything with friends here. Sorry, little lady, pretend I didn't—"

Ubi turned to the maid, smiling—then recognized the girl's face, and froze.

"H-hi, not a girl. Definitely a boy. Lloyd Belladonna. Haven't seen you since the wrap party on that movie that never came out."

"......I'm *so* sorry, Natie."

Ubi had never imagined he was right here, in drag.

Mena was way past the capacity for speech. All color had drained from her face.

"Mm? Mena, what's wrong? You've gone white as a sheet!" Lloyd said, shaking her shoulder.

She finally breathed again. "L-L-Lloyd! That was just my mom's... idea of a joke."

"Don't worry! It's my fault for dressing like this. Ubi, don't worry about it."

"N-n-not my concern! It's the second half!"

"Second half? Sorry, I was so distracted by her thinking I was a girl I didn't hear anything after that."

And since he hadn't heard anything about "telling Lloyd how you feel," he'd quietly recovered from the shock of mistaken gender identity.

©Nao Watanuki

"What did she say...wait, 'Mom'? Mena, are you...?"

"Oops."

"Are you and Mina related? You know, I thought there was a resemblance!"

"...Um."

Lloyd's instincts were clearly not getting any better.

"Well, let Mina know I'd love to see her again, and I'm looking forward to her next movie! Oh...I should probably explain that I was calling myself Roy..."

During filming, he'd used rune magic to make himself look older—and that wasn't helping him sort out his thoughts.

And the particular phrase he'd chosen left Mina/Mena's head spinning—and her eyes!

Just when her mortification reached its peak—

"I'm not feeling well, so I'm going on break! Take over for me!" she yelled, and she ran off.

"Um, what's happened to Mena?" Lloyd said.

Sardin patted him on the head.

"Don't you worry about it," he said. "We'll welcome you into our family anytime."

Lloyd had no idea what that could possibly mean.

While the lovey-dovey (LOL) royal couple were spreading good cheer, the top diplomat was nearby, asking questions.

The soldiers investigating the statue theft had not expected anyone on his level to be personally involved in the field and could not conceal their surprise.

"I suppose it *has* been a while... Most of my time is spent stuck behind a desk or dispatched to foreign lands."

Still, seeing shocked looks on the faces of every passing soldier made him wince.

"We were made of sterner stuff in my day! You don't know how easy you have it. In my job, a single failure means years of hard work before anyone trusts you again."

Sighing, he thought fondly of his youth.

He'd been on vacation in Rokujou and had met young Sardin—and had been so desperate to make a connection that the whole thing had blown up in his face. Even now, he had countless people slaving away, trying to restore the relationship between the two countries.

"I mistook Prince Sardin for a fool and tried to butter him up—he sure had my number. If I'd just been straight with the man, said my piece like that Lloyd boy did, perhaps everything would have been different."

That cadet had really made an impression on him.

An earnest face, plainspoken, the gumption to speak his mind to a superior...years of experience negotiating with allies and merchants alike made it clear to the diplomat that Lloyd was an honest soul.

"Sometimes that kind of sincerity is what you need! But I suppose there's no use dwelling on it now. Argh, discovering how that fool of a prince was actually brilliant will haunt me the rest of my... Oh?"

His eyes had just lit upon Lloyd himself—that maid garb *really* stood out.

The diplomat thought nothing of calling out to him.

"Young Lloyd, how goes the investigation?"

"Oh, sir! Working on it now!"

Lloyd saluted him, and the diplomat's eyes turned to the people in his company.

"Glad to hear it. And these would be—" His voice died in his throat.

There stood the source of his youthful folly—Sardin himself, in disguise.

The look on the diplomat's face was enough for Sardin to place him, and he lowered his sunglasses, greeting him.

"You're that diplomat of Azami, yes? It's been a while."

"Th-that it has, Your Majesty. I apologize for interrupting your time away."

"Not at all. The festival has been a delight."

"......"

"......"

Given their history, once the bare minimum of small talk concluded, it was difficult for these two to sustain the conversation.

Ubi and Lloyd exchanged puzzled glances.

"You're never at a loss for words," she said. "What's going on?"

"Oh, just…"

Given the man's previously blatant obsequious manner, he'd maintained a careful distance—and didn't want to dig that up now.

The diplomatic liaison was equally at a loss.

"Are you okay?" Lloyd asked. "You've gone rather pale."

The diplomat looked at him and remembered his thought from a moment before.

"Sincerity. And the gumption to speak your mind."

He took a deep breath and turned to Sardin, bowing his head.

"King Sardin, allow me to offer a belated apology for my disgraceful behavior back in the day. I shamed myself and my country."

Sardin had not expected a man in his position to offer an apology at all, let alone for something in the distant past.

"It was a long time ago!" he said. "I've long since forgotten. But what brought this on?"

The diplomat smiled. "I've long wanted to apologize, but my position stood in the way. And the boy here helped remind me of that lingering desire."

He clapped a hand on Lloyd's shoulder.

Sardin got it at once, smiling broadly. A real smile—not a professional one.

"Aha! He does that."

Sensing deeper meaning behind this, the diplomat asked, "You seemed quite friendly. You've met before?"

Lowering his voice so Lloyd couldn't hear, Sardin replied, "Just between the two of us, I'd happily let him marry my daughter."

"A-and leave Rokujou in his hands?!"

"Yes, he's already saved us once. Although the boy himself doesn't realize it…you've noticed already how direct and pure of heart he is. I think he'd make an excellent king."

Sardin spoke with an impish grin that made it hard to tell if he was joking or not.

There was a faint smile on Ubi's lips as well. "He'd be a better one than you, clearly."

"Darling! You cut me to the quick!"

He tried to snuggle up, and she pushed him away, glancing up at the clock tower.

"Right, right…we're out of time. Later, Lloyd."

"Oh, right! I'm sure we'll meet again," he said to the diplomat. "And Lloyd—ciao."

He waved dramatically, and the royal couple walked away. Lloyd watched them go, then the diplomat turned to him.

"Lloyd, wasn't it? Do you have a career in mind? A placement you'd like?"

"No, not in particular."

"Well, if you're ever interested in diplomacy, we'd be glad to have you."

Lloyd's eyes went wide. "Huh? M-me?"

"The times no longer call for calculations and second guessing. We need people like you as well. I look forward to your answer."

He patted the boy on his shoulders and went away, smiling happily.

"D-did he mean that?" Lloyd wondered. "I suppose I *should* figure out my future…but first, I've got a patrol to finish, and a sculpture to find."

Fired up, Lloyd went out hunting for the Statue of Love.

Left on his own, Lloyd took over Mena's security position.

But they'd exchanged absolutely no notes on what that involved, so Lloyd was unclear what he was even supposed to be doing. He just wound up keeping an eye out for anyone suspicious…while being flummoxed by the looks his outfit drew.

And one person watching him was equally at a loss.

"Why, though…?"

Here was the boy, Shouma. He had just assumed Lloyd would change to go on patrol and had been waiting this whole time for his chance to get good footage, but the maid thing persevered!

"Does this mean he's starting to *like* that outfit? Some things are best left for the privacy of your own home!"

A thought loaded with problems.

Shouma was stationed up a tree, but decided he couldn't stand idly by and jumped out, landing next to Lloyd like a flying squirrel.

Lloyd jumped a foot in the air. "Augh?! A criminal?"

"Glad to see you've still got the heart of a soldier, Lloyd! Keep that passion!"

"Oh, Shouma."

"That's right, little brother! Been ages since we met face-to-face."

Realizing he knew the intruder, Lloyd breathed a sigh of relief. "You startled me... Wait, Shouma, are you still dealing with him? The man they call Sou?"

"Mm? Old man Sou? Yep, we're still thick as thieves."

"You can't do that! He's a bad influence! At least go back home sometimes; everyone's worried about you."

Shouma was on his knees, listening intently. Smiling.

"Sorry, Lloyd! I'll go home when the time's right. And I know Sou looks shady, but he's a good guy. Just...right now, he's got a goal and is forcing himself to do bad things to achieve it."

"Even Chief Alka said he's bad news!"

"...He's just a little lost. But! That's not the real problem! Your clothes are! Do you *like* them?!"

"N-no! Definitely not. Everyone's staring, and it's really awkward."

Lloyd explained that their butler clothes had gone missing, and then his uniform had vanished.

"And you've checked Selen's things?"

Everyone's top suspect.

"I'm sure someone just took it to the lost and found."

Shouma folded his arms, considering this. "If it's not Selen, then the chief's the second suspect...but there may be some as-yet-unknown dire third party involved. Either way, we've gotta get that back ASAP."

"Um, Shouma?"

Shouma made up his mind and shot Lloyd a thumbs-up. "Don't worry, Lloyd! I'll be right back with your uniform, for you and your future!"

"My future? Please. At worst, I'll have to say I'm sorry and ask for a new one."

But Shouma's smile just got broader.

"The future is never far away! Actions today come back tomorrow! The whole world will soon know your name! Trust me."

And he was gone like the wind.

"Wait… Man, nobody could ever pin him down."

Shouma began searching for Lloyd's uniform, dead certain he'd find it soon.

"We've gotta make a world where Lloyd's efforts pay off! A world where his good deeds are rewarded. Just you wait! I'll make this a world worth saving, so you can be a hero they'll talk about for generations."

As Shouma ran off…Zalko was wearing Lloyd's uniform, in a warehouse with the kidnapped king, looking extremely baffled.

"I *am* king, right?"

"Don't ask *me*!"

"Did I do something wrong? I can't imagine why they'd ignore me like this—do I have bad breath?!"

"I'm as lost as you are!"

Their positions had reversed themselves. Now the king was anxiously fretting away, and Zalko was getting rather annoyed and increasingly unsure of himself.

Two in a row looked right at him, pretended he wasn't there! And nobody came back!

He'd been ready to run once Phyllo left, but there were still no signs of anyone surrounding them.

I figured I'd run once they made their move, but how can I do that if they don't do anything? This is a first! Wait, is this all part of their cunning plan?!

Unable to predict the Azami army's next move, Zalko increased his estimation of their strategy, when in actual fact, they simply were unaware that the king had been kidnapped.

Ignoring the king's moans, Zalko buried himself in thought, eventually reaching a conclusion—*Oh! He must be the king's double!*

Quite a misunderstanding.

But human brains are wired to concoct supporting evidence once a conclusion has been reached. Zalko thought it explained everything.

Naturally! There were no guards at all—and they'd never be acting so calm after a kidnapping, otherwise! This geezer's just doing his job!

"Are you listening? Does nobody listen to the king anymore?"

And the moment he thought I was onto him, he started babbling, trying to pull the wool over my eyes!

"Hello?"

Those two soldiers were just checking where I was… They plan to kill me and *the double! With a bomb, or…? What kind of country is this?!*

Whatever kind of country killed hostages and captors, Azami was now it.

Meanwhile, the actual king of this despotic hellhole was in tears.

"Heed the word of your king!"

"Damn, you're a fake! You had me fooled!"

"Er, what? No? You kidnapped *me!*"

"And you want to keep me in the blast radius? I've been in this game a decade! I'm not so easily fooled!"

"Blast radius? Is something going to blow up?"

The king was not keeping up with Zalko's inner delusions.

Zalko quickly grabbed his things and raced to the door.

"You're leaving me here?! Abandoning your hostage?!"

"Yep, sorry! If I'm with you, my life is forfeit!"

"Did you think of that before kidnapping the king?! *Hngg!*"

Worried about the noise, Zalko had put his gag back on. "Not wasting another second on a double…," he muttered, heading for the door again.

"Mmmphhhh!"

The king was trying to say, "What, abandoning me? Now you're ignoring me, too? Whyyy?" but the gag ruined it.

His muffled groan echoed through the storeroom.

Outside, Zalko scratched his head, wondering what to do next.

"Can't believe I grabbed a double by accident… I underestimated Azami."

He glanced at the position of the sun and made up his mind.

"Guess I'll just nab the real one! Scope out the soldiers' movements, locate his position…that's a job worth doing."

And with that, Zalko headed out to search for the "real" king—who was still trussed up behind him.

Little did he know just what horrors lay in his future.

Once Shouma left, Lloyd kept working security in his maid outfit, but was running out of steam.

"Hmm…what does 'suspicious' really mean?"

Lloyd was truly struggling. Everyone who saw him was giving him looks of great curiosity, and this was making it hard to tell "suspicious" from "auspicious."

"I suppose my best bet is to look anywhere a statue might be hidden…and hope the others find the butler garb and my uniform."

"……Mm."

"! Augh! Ph-Phyllo?!"

Maid Phyllo had appeared behind him unexpectedly. Her training in the Ascorbic Domain seemed to have given her a newfound knack for stealth.

She looked down at him, not a glimmer of expression showing.

"……I agree."

"Agree with what? Something up with the maid café?"

"…Low on ingredients, so I'm buying more. And I found you." Phyllo held up two bags of groceries. "……I agree with moving."

"So you're looking for the statue, too?"

"……Also that."

"But mostly?"

"……I want to see the festival with you."

Her arm locked with Lloyd's.

"Um, Phyllo? Why'd you take my arm? Are we doing grappling practice dressed like *this*?"

"………Umm…"

She gave him a look that said, *No?* and then dragged him to a nearby stall.

The two of them walking arm in arm was quite a picture, and the crowd was abuzz.

"Phyllo, are we *not* searching for the statue?"

"......I think you need to relax, Master. I know you've been all fired up since we appointed you head of our class. But...it's too much."

He fell silent, aware that she had a point.

"......And if we act natural, our foe might slip up."

"True. Okay, let's tour the festival a bit. Act normally, see if we can find anything that way."

Phyllo nodded and tugged his arm again.

"But I don't know if standing this close is *natural...*"

"......I'm hungry. They're selling something over there. Let's go look."

"Uh, Phyllo?"

"......Act natural."

She kept saying that, but she wasn't loosening her grip on him at all. Cunning.

Unable to muster further arguments, Lloyd was pulled toward the stall.

Soon after, they could hear food frying over the noise of the crowd.

Then the breeze flitting through the foot traffic carried the scent of savory sauce and seaweed... Voices everywhere were filled with delight, but this area was extra buoyant—like this was the source of the festival cheer.

"That smells good!"

Phyllo merely nodded. Then her stomach rumbled—and she didn't look remotely embarrassed.

"......I can't wait," she admitted.

Lloyd smiled and pointed ahead. "Then you choose. I was too busy with our stuff and don't really know what else there is."

"......That's a shame. Leave it to me."

Phyllo pulled out a pamphlet and held it open for him. She'd drawn red lines all over it, so clearly she had been looking forward to this.

"......I'm curious about this one."

She was pointing at the supply transportation team's extra-filling onigiri. The rice was stuffed with salty fillings, and the balls formed were the size of a child's head.

"Whoa, Phyllo…that's exactly the sort of stall I'd want to check out."

"……Yes, my research suggested as much."

"Your…research?"

"……The more you know about the one you love," she whispered.

It was almost drowned out by the noise of the crowd, but Lloyd's ears caught some of it.

"Mm? What? Love?"

He caught the word but not the intent.

"……Do I have to say it again?"

Her expression never changed, but…her cheeks were definitely red. And the heated look she gave him betrayed a blend of stress and anxiety.

Was this the right time to tell him?

Phyllo's training had taught her that giving up only did her harm, so she took a deep breath and forced herself to speak.

"……………I lo—"

"Mwa-ha-ha! Fancy meeting you here! Tiger abs stand proud at our reunion!"

Phyllo's resolve was demolished by a guttural male bellow.

They turned to find—a forty-something man in bikini briefs, a masquerade mask, and a cape, muscles bulging everywhere. It was the chief of the Ascorbic Domain's Tiger clan, Tiger Nexamic, performing a traditional clan greeting that enhanced his glutes and hamstrings.

A half-naked man accosting two maids—clear probable cause.

"Oh, Tiger Nexamic. It's been a while."

"Lloyd, my boy! You've kept in shape!"

"I train as much as my feeble body allows!"

"Mwa-ha-ha, you use *Aero* to fly, yet are too oblivious to realize your own strength. But you make it work! Keep building that confidence and be a man I can be proud to count as a friend. What's wrong, Phyllo Quinone? You wiped the floor with me! That look of defeat does not suit you."

"……You're a different kind of oblivious."

The kind that interrupted a romantic confession with a butt flex. Even with her poker face, Phyllo was *clearly* furious.

"Oblivious? Moi? True! My hamstrings have reached a level of appeal even I cannot fathom! The unconscious allure of the oblivious muscle!"

But as always, this grown-ass man never listened to *anyone*. He simply ran through his repertoire of flexes, asking, "But why the fancy dress? Skirts do flaunt the hamstrings, but not as well as my tight shorts!"

".........We're running a maid café."

"Aha! And this is your break? I've interrupted your date! Alas."

"Oh, no, Nexamic. This isn't a date; it's a security patrol."

"......You're both depressingly dense."

Buffeted from both sides—Nexamic just calling it a date out loud, and Lloyd being forced to deny it—even Phyllo was starting to look visibly frustrated.

"Allow me to buy you a meal, by way of apology. This way!"

Nexamic glute-guided them along.

"......Where, exactly?"

"Naturally, to my own stall! Or rather...*our* stall!"

He pointed ahead to a packed throng. At the center of the crowd...

"Yakisoba with plenty of organic cabbage! A perfect pairing with the wheat grown in my village!"

A man wearing nothing but a headband and a loincloth was working the grill, dishing up a stir-fried noodle dish.

"E-ex-Colonel Merthophan!"

This man had fallen prey to a demon lord's tricks, and to make up for it, he had devoted himself to Kunlun village farming. That was now his primary enthusiasm, and he'd returned to Azami as an agricultural advisor—but as ex-military, he'd been asked to open a stall here.

"On that fateful day, I realized the path to true muscle lay in fieldwork. I've been serving as Brother Merthophan's aide, traveling to many lands."

Nexamic discarded his cape, donning a matching headband. This being a festival, it was mildly less outlandish looking, but Phyllo was unclear what part of yakisoba required near nudity.

"...There's zero point in doing that in the buff."

"N-now, now, Phyllo, he's allowed to do what he wants," Lloyd said.

Merthophan heard them and came over. "Been a while. Glad to see you both doing well."

"Far too long, ex-Colonel."

"......Same."

Merthophan glanced over their maid outfits but only winced a little. "Your dress... Chrome failed to supervise the festival properly, I see. Allowed Riho Flavin to run toward the profit horizon?"

He was right on the money, and they both clapped.

""......Wow.""

"Really, just because it's a festival doesn't mean you can wear anything!"

Coming from a man in a loincloth, this was not convincing.

Another man was watching all this from a distance.

"An odd assembly," he muttered.

It was Zalko. Certain he'd been bamboozled by a double, he was out searching for the real king—and had located the former army commander, Merthophan. A big enough name to stake out.

"The former leader of the Azami's war hawks, Merthophan Dextro—meeting with what I assume are cadets from the military school."

And they were in disguise, no less. Zalko was unaware that the uniforms he himself had stolen had forced them to dress as maids.

"Maids, a loincloth...and a powerfully built stranger. Is he a soldier, too? They must be exchanging information on the down low. I should get closer and listen in."

Careful to keep himself hidden, Zalko sneaked across the grass until he was right alongside them.

Now then, what are they talking about?

He perked up his ears just as Merthophan and Lloyd started chatting about Kunlun.

"Is Satan getting along with everyone back in Kunlun?"

"Far better than I ever did. I mean...he's not *human*, but..."

"But?"

"He's very human-like? I feel like he must have been human once."

"Satan was a human?!"

"Yeah, and when I asked the chief about it, she got real evasive. She said she'd be attending the festival, so you should ask her yourself."

Zalko was immediately lost.

What the…? Some sort of code? Kunlun's the village from the fairy tales, right?

Wrong. It was a totally normal conversation to anyone actually from the place, but…did not sound that way to outside ears.

Zalko listened even closer.

Phyllo was just standing there, watching them talk…likely dwelling on her interrupted confession, frustrated that she couldn't get back to it, thinking thoughts like, *Why did you just let that slip out?* and *Why didn't you just say it loud and clear?*

Very much being a teenager, in other words.

Nexamic picked up on this, and his traps rippled as he leaned in.

"That look on your face…," he whispered. "Are you gearing up to ask him out?"

"……!"

He'd gone straight for the jugular.

And the look on her face was *highly* out of character.

"Ha-ha-ha! I jest. A little Tiger ☆ Joke!"

"———!" Phyllo was never good at letting her emotions show. At a loss for where to vent them, she made a fist and punched Nexamic as hard as she could.

Facing herself in the Ascorbic Domain had left Phyllo with newfound mental fortitude and an awareness of her own romantic desires—and also had clearly upped the force of her swing.

"Mwa-ha! Why violence?!"

A beautiful uppercut. A forty-something lump of meat flying through the air, bewildered. Unaware of how richly deserved this was, he landed butt-first on the grass—

Right on top of Zalko.

"Huh? Why'd that girl hit the bodybuilder…? Wow, that's some air—wait…"

The whole sequence had left him stunned, and he just watched Nexamic arc through the air.

And before he knew it, he was buried in the man's butt.

"Gah!"

"Mwa-ha! A surprise attack! But my flexibility allowed me to land unharmed upon my rear end! Mm?"

His guffaw died down as he noticed Zalko writhing beneath his posterior.

"G-get your butt off my...face! The acrid...stench!"

"Oh, my apologizes, Soldier. Are you harmed? Should I carry you to the med ward?"

The fleshy butt stomp had certainly left Zalko's eyes totally dead.

Reeling from damage less physical than mental, he staggered to his feet and waved the muscleman off.

Y-you ass! You sensed me watching and put on a charade of being hit so you could land a pinpoint blow on me. And now you're trying to use this med ward crap as an excuse to arrest me? Just take anyone suspicious into custody, no questions asked? Is that how Azami does things?

"I'm fine," he said and ran off like a bat out of hell.

"Something wrong, Nexamic?"

"Oh, Lloyd! I may have butt-stomped that poor soldier. For some reason, he fled when I tried to apologize!"

"......Anyone would."

"So...why *did* you punch him, Phyllo?"

"Quite the payback for a harmless little joke...ah-ha! You saw the functionality returning to muscular beauty, and the fighter in you could not resist!"

"Oh, was that it? Even if you're aching to fight him, you should really warn him first, Phyllo."

"......Obliviousness makes it so hard."

Phyllo clutched her head. Lloyd's romance route was blocked by his own cluelessness.

"......I will overcome!"

The higher the obstacle, the more you wanted to scale it. Lloyd was her target, both as a martial artist and as a marital prospect.

"Don't be silly, Phyllo! You have already overcome my muscles!"

Concluding that further conversation was futile, Phyllo silently took a bite of her noodles.

Merthophan called for him, and Nexamic went back to the grill—but Lloyd and Phyllo weren't left alone for long.

The new face was of average height and build, dressed like a nobleman. His eyes sloped downward like a forlorn puppy, and his hair was a tangled mass that defied the beholder's ability to tell if it naturally grew that way or if someone had actually meant it to look like that.

Lloyd's face lit up instantly.

"Oh! Satan!"

"Mm? Lloyd, fancy meeting you here—and wearing…"

The maid thing really rattled Satan, and especially since Lloyd had been so happy to see him he'd reached out and grabbed Satan's hands. Objective solicitation.

"……Go on." Phyllo finished a noodle slurp, watching how this played out.

"I think you have a lot of things to reconsider, Lloyd. What is this?!"

"Oh, sorry, I should explain. I was just so happy to see my master again!"

Satan clearly still wasn't comfortable with that title.

He'd been operating as the demon lord of the night and as part of Eug's conspiracy. Until recently, he'd had no memories of being human, but events had conspired to leave him training Lloyd—convinced the boy wished to be his minion. Though still superhuman, he was no longer acting all evil and was just like the cool older dude next door.

Satan looked from Lloyd to Phyllo and then figured it out.

"So you're doing a maid café? That the gist of it, Phyllo?"

"……Yep."

Not what he'd expected from the Military Festival.

"Riho's idea?" Satan asked, chuckling. "No matter what's happened to the world, if you go for the basest instincts, you rake it in. Oh, what a world."

He scratched his head, then took another look at them.

"Am I interrupting anything?" he asked.

"Not at all," Lloyd said, shaking his head. "I'm glad you found the time to visit! You're my only master, Satan!"

Satan winced and gave Phyllo a look of pity. "You poor thing," he said, well aware of how she felt.

"......Mm."

Possibly it was the most loaded "Mm" she'd ever mustered. Loving Lloyd was a constant struggle.

Oblivious to this, Lloyd just kept demonstrating his mastery of the "cute but dumb" archetype.

"Did you just get here, Satan?"

"Yep. Alka made me haul this weird thing here from the village."

"......Weird thing?"

"It was pretty gnarly looking, so probably a ward against evil? She had me deposit it in Marie's house. So I figured I'd scope out the town, and wound up here."

"Wow, that sounds rough."

Satan just shrugged it off. "She's always been demanding, you know? Not just Alka—the lab chief was even worse! Demanding I edit videos of her clearing games one-handed or without saves."

As Satan drifted into memory, Phyllo's head tipped to one side. "......Without saves?"

"Oh, sorry, Phyllo. Not a phrase that still has meaning."

No use talking about games this fantasy world no longer had.

But something seemed to be jogging Lloyd's memory. "Mm?" he said.

"What's up, Lloyd?"

"Not saving...games? Where have I heard that before?"

Shocked, Satan grabbed his shoulders. "Y-you've heard it?! If we can find the lab chief, we might find out what really happened and how to put the world back the way it was! Anything you can tell me, anything at all!"

"S-Satan, you're shaking me!"

Satan saw Lloyd looking unwell and quickly let go.

"Uh, s-sorry," he stammered.

"......Crime in progress."

"Phyllo! No, seriously, I really am sorry." He recovered somewhat, bowing his head to her as well.

"......What's this about, Satan?"

Looking guilty, he scratched his head, choosing his words carefully.

"Um, I'm trying to find a person who used those words a lot. Anything would help, no matter how small."

Lloyd rubbed his forehead, thinking hard. "Um, I think it was in the bathroom, in the Domain."

"Bathroom? But it was a woman, right?"

"Oh, yes. It was dark, so I didn't get a good look…"

"Par for the course with her, really. Tony once called her the patron saint of free spirits. Anyway, sorry again."

Lloyd shook his head. "No, it's all right. But we'd better be going— we've got a lot to do. Sorry I couldn't show you around."

"……Mm."

"Don't worry about it. I did notice the soldiers were rushing about— something going on?"

Lloyd and Phyllo glanced at each other and decided to fill him in.

"Actually, a statue on loan from Profen—"

They explained how Zalko had stolen the statue. Satan's expression grew grimmer by the minute.

"A…statue, you say?"

"…It vanished into thin air. This morning."

"The morning… And you said it was made from stone? That's about when Alka showed up with… Oh god."

"What's wrong, Satan?"

"Mm? Uh, never mind. I'll help look. I might have a lead."

"…That's…good news."

Satan waved and headed off toward the Central District.

"But that hideous thing can't be the Statue of Love…and why would Alka steal it? But…what *else* could it be?"

Having seen the statue himself, he found the name hard to believe.

"I mean, it's a piece of junk! Nothing about it says 'love.'"

…Go ahead and cry, Alka.

Lloyd and Phyllo wished Nexamic and Merthophan luck enjoying the festival and left. Working his way through his helping of yakisoba, Lloyd looked around.

"The only weird person I've seen was that soldier looking for the statue in the grass."

So he *had* spotted Zalko…and then proceeded to completely ignore him. As he remained vigilant, something came bounding through the trees—was it even human?!

"Mm? Who could that—? Oh!"

"Sir Llooooooyd! There you aaaaaare!"

Selen, naturally. She didn't really count as human anymore. She'd left that behind.

She'd clearly ditched her post, still in her maid clothes, and was gliding around like a flying squirrel using arcane olfactory talents to locate Lloyd. She landed cleanly and moved swiftly into a tackle that would make a rugby player blanch. Her dive was clearly aimed to go right under Lloyd's maid skirts—a level of sexual harassment that was very forceful.

But Phyllo spotted her coming and stepped in, blocking the dive with a well-timed chop.

"I-impressive, Phyllo."

"……Your tenacity is admirable. But no matter how hard you push those legs, I won't budge."

Selen was working those quads like an American football player on a tackling sled.

The belt on her hips shook its buckle. "Mistress, best you stop flailing and state your intentions."

Vritra's voice finally moved her out of perpetual tackle mode.

"That's an excellent suggestion! Phyllo, I've got a message for you."

"……For me?"

"Yes! Your parents came by."

"……They threatened to," Phyllo said, nodding.

"They meant to visit after greeting the king, but couldn't find him, so seemed rather at a loss. With the statue search, nobody really has time to sit with them, so we're hoping you can do the honors."

"……If it was just Dad, I'd rather not…but Mom's with him?"

She scratched her head, then turned to look.

"......Master, I've gotta run. It was fun."

"Don't worry, Phyllo! I'll take over entertaining Sir Lloyd."

"......That's extremely worrying."

"Hurry along! That king was in tears."

Phyllo could easily picture Sardin weeping openly.

"......That dumb dandy..."

Reluctantly, she headed off toward the castle.

Selen gave a triumphant smile, as if her rivals were dealt with. From many angles, this would look positively diabolical.

"Come, Sir Lloyd! You must tour the festival with me, too. Phyllo can't have all the fun."

"Uh, Selen...I'm still on security duty. We're searching for the statue or Zalko. And aren't you working the shop?"

"The course of my life is entirely up to me."

She was so firm that Lloyd decided fighting was useless.

"Okay, then," he said. "I'll hang out with you some, but don't forget our real goal."

"I see! You were just 'hanging out' with Phyllo, but *I'm* your 'real goal.'"

The words passed through the interpretive filter in Selen's mind, emerging with a spin in her favor.

"You can't just assign new meanings to words! Our goal is the statue and anyone acting suspicious!"

Lloyd gave it his best shot, but Selen's smile was indomitable.

"I know! Same as before."

"Before?"

"Our date at Reiyoukaku! We were searching for clues to the coma case, while acting like we were on a date."

"R-right. I was there."

"I remember it like yesterday! It *was* our first date." She put her hand in his, squeezing tight.

"S-Selen!"

"You did this with Phyllo."

"No, that's not the problem—I mean, last time we pretended to date, we never actually found any clues, and Riho wound up doing all the work."

"I have forgotten that inconvenient detail! Come on!"

Nothing could stop Selen now, and Vritra was forced to apologize in full capable boss mode.

"Pray forgive her, Lloyd. We shall provide what assistance we can, so allow her to do things her way."

Lloyd sheepishly nodded and let Selen lead him off toward a new stall. Specifically—

"The intelligence bureau's fortune-telling booth?"

The espionage agency was running a stall that read palms and told couples if they were compatible.

"Precisely! Experienced spies are excellent judges of character! They don't rely on birthdates alone! They use their knowledge of physiognomy, statistics, and psychology to predict if a relationship will work out, with ninety percent accuracy!"

"Ninety?! That's incredible!"

"Unfortunately, they're soldiers by trade, so they don't really mince words."

Just as Selen dropped that fact, a woman raced past, weeping, a flustered man hot on her heels.

"I was a fool to trust you!"

"Wait! How can physiognomy prove I'm a gold digger?!"

"Part of me knew all along! You were always so interested in my fortune! You're never available when I ask you on a date! And when you invite me, it's always about money!"

"Please! I'm definitely short on cash, but that's just *part* of your appeal!"

The fortune-teller's notorious bluntness may not have been the problem. Several men in line visibly flinched, realizing that this shop's "fortune-telling" amounted to hiring a private detective.

"*Is* this technically fortune-telling?"

"That was an exception, I'm sure. Oh?"

They spotted a familiar face near the door.

"Colonel Choline?"

She seemed to be waiting for someone and turned eagerly toward them.

"You're late—oh, it's just you."

"Why so jumpy, Colonel? Lots of suspicious activity here?"

"Aw, no. I'm searching, but I had a prior engagement here, so…"

She clearly didn't want to talk about it, but Lloyd just happily asked anyway.

"Oh? With who?"

"Uh, so…"

"Pardon the delay, Choline."

They turned toward this new voice and found Merthophan—wearing a white T-shirt and canvas pants like a normal person.

"Colonel Merthophan!"

He seemed surprised to see Lloyd and Selen.

"We meet again, Lloyd. But what manner of stall is this?" He looked up at the fortune-telling stall, perplexed.

Choline made a face and had a furious internal debate about whether to explain herself.

"Erm, well…," she stammered.

But Selen jumped ahead of her, giving her teacher a friendly pat on the shoulders.

"Eh-heh-heh! I completely understand, Colonel Choline. Like myself, you seek divination."

She mouthed "romantic," and Choline blushed, nodding.

"That obvious? But yeah, basically same goal as you."

"Indeed. I fully expect them to declare us destined partners and go, 'Well, they'll just have to get married, then!' and have him sign the certificate."

Basically brainwashing.

Choline's plan had been far more realistic, so she shot Selen a horrified look, and then shook her head.

"The first half is right anyway. 'Course, then the problem is…what if they tell us we're a bad match?"

"Don't worry! I have complete confidence."

"You're confident."

They all got in line and moved into the shop's interior.

It was just a simple sign saying FORTUNE-TELLING outside a classroom entrance. The interior was largely unchanged as well—no fancy decorations. They'd simply partitioned it off to handle multiple clients at a time—like an office, or the counter at a bank.

Despite the partitions, voices carried; people were asking about love, losing their virginity, or how to pay back their loans. Some…pretty critical stuff here. Especially the latter two.

"Looks like it isn't *just* couples."

"Yes, love is not the only matter that preys on the mind," Merthophan said, completely missing the point.

Choline sighed. "If only you knew what preyed on mine."

"Then share it with me. Frankly, I'm unclear why we're here at all!"

As she sighed again, their number was called. The four of them moved to a window together.

This one section of the room *did* go for the fortune-teller look; the woman at the counter had an embroidered purple hood and a crystal ball in front of her.

"Thou art my next lost lambs—"

She spoke in an archaic style that definitely put you in the mood to have your fortune read.

"Wow, she must be good. She's dressed like Marie!"

"The decor is a letdown, but at least the mystic is a pro."

Merthophan was not one to let a vibe go unshattered, though.

"Ah, you're the intelligence division's—"

"The wheels of fate—oh, ex-Colonel Merthophan! It's been ages!"

The mystic vibe dissipated instantly. It was a military-run affair; of course everyone knew each other. The fortune-teller dropped her hood to salute, and Merthophan returned the gesture.

"Why is he like this?" Choline moaned.

"Oh, Colonel Choline and two cadets? Are you sure you all want to go together? It doesn't get cheaper."

"Not an issue. Still, never been to your bureau's stall before. You dress the part but don't decorate accordingly?"

"Yeah, honestly; these outfits were our entire budget. Nothing left to decorate with…"

Lloyd and Selen both made faces—this sort of behind-the-scenes intel was best kept secret.

Spotting this, the fortune-teller quickly reassured them. "No biggie," she said—definitely not a phrase used by someone prone to saying "thou."

"Intelligence work means doing cold reads is a vital skill. The kind of problems people take to fortune-tellers usually lead pretty easily to the right answer. Like you, for instance."

She pointed at Lloyd, and he jumped.

"Me?!"

"You've got problems, right? Lemme see your hand."

He offered it up, and she took it, looking it over. One finger on his pulse, she looked up at his face.

"Um…?"

"Love…no, health? No…work… Aha! That's what's troubling you."

"Is this the third degree?"

Lie detectors measured pulses, not fortune-tellers.

"You may not notice, but your pulse *does* shift. We can read your palms, hear what you have to say, and help you out. So what is your work concern?"

"I-I'm trying to decide where to go after school."

Merthophan and Choline both looked surprised.

"Lloyd, you're still a first-year! A bit soon, isn't it?"

He scratched his cheek sheepishly. "Yes, I know I've got time to figure it out. But I saw how hard the second-years are working, and I started fretting."

"Hmm."

"I enlisted to be a soldier like the one in my favorite novel, but… that's not really a career path."

"Even within the army there are roles as disparate as 'royal guard' or 'diplomatic liaison.' I'm sure you'll have people lining up to take you. Intelligence work pays well! I recommend it."

The fortune-teller thumped her chest, her performance long since forgotten.

"That's certainly true, Lloyd. My plans are already set!"

"Really? That's amazing, Selen."

He gave her a look of deep respect.

Everyone else—even the fortune-teller—immediately assumed she meant "Lloyd's wife."

"All I can really tell you is to think about it long and hard," the fortune-teller said, rolling her crystal ball across the desk. "Make good use of your time and figure out what kind of soldier you want to be. Talk to your friends, your teachers, and your superior officers, do trial experiences at different workplaces—experience is everything."

There was just nothing divinatory about this at all now. But it seemed to be what Lloyd needed to hear, and he looked very grateful.

"Thank you so much! I'll make I sure I don't regret anything."

Merthophan gave his back a gentle pat. "That's the spirit, Lloyd! It's not a question of choosing the right path, it's a question of putting in the work to make the best of the path you've chosen. I expect great things."

"Yes, sir!" Lloyd replied, super upbeat.

"You've got a good one there, ex-Colonel," the fortune-teller laughed.

Merthophan looked pleased. "He'll be an asset to the army's might and a viable successor to me on Kunlun's farms."

"And we're back to agriculture." Choline sighed.

"And for you two?" the fortune-teller asked, turning to her. "Compatibility?"

"Mm...nah, forget it. Good reminder why it is I love him, and like you said—you gotta put in the work to make the path you choose work."

"Mm? What was that, Choline?"

"! Forget you heard anything! You big lug."

"Eh-heh-heh, I don't need to read anything to know you're meant for each other."

The fortune-teller grinned, but just as everything seemed to reach a happy conclusion...

"I want to reaffirm my own position! I demand our compatibility in cold hard numbers I can use to silence any foe."

Selen ruined everything.

"Ah-ha-ha, she's a standout, too. Okay, sit thouself down afore the crystal."

She was really half-assing this archaic thing, but Lloyd and Selen took their seats.

"Fill in the necessary fields here...yes, and there..."

Muttering, she checked over the documents, comparing them...not using the crystal at all...

"Is this just decorative?"

"Basically. We're calling it fortune-telling, but it's really just using the intelligence department's vast profiling resources to figure you kids out and see if you'll work together, which is way more accurate."

"Gosh, spies can do anything," Lloyd said.

"Eh-heh-heh!" Selen cackled. "This profiling will undoubtedly prove we're meant for each other one hundred percent! No, one hundred and twenty percent! And why stop there? Two hundred percent! Double the mutuals! I cannot wait."

Lloyd just looked lost, and Merthophan and Choline were shaking their heads.

Meanwhile, the fortune-teller was muttering to herself.

"...Yeesh, what a mess."

"........." Selen's ears caught that, and she was momentarily petrified. Possibly fossilized.

Then her head turned to the fortune-teller with an audible screech, eyes hollow.

"......Did I hear the word 'mess' or do my ears deceive me?"

The fortune-teller scratched her eyebrow, at a loss. "Uh...brace yourself?"

"Brace myself? Our compatibility is shockingly good, then? I see!"

Selen was clearly not prepared to accept any bad news.

The fortune-teller swiveled to Merthophan, seeking guidance.

"We're running out of time, so just get it over with. No matter how disastrous the results."

She gasped at the resolve in his voice...looking less like a fortune-teller than a judge about to pronounce a sentence.

"Listen well."

"Oh, sure!" Lloyd said, not really thinking hard about it.

Selen took two deep breaths like a judo champ training up a mountain, then said, "Hit me." This was clearly not how you prepared for an unknown outcome. She knew it was bad.

"Lloyd, Selen, your compatibility is…"

"Yes…"

"Ten…"

"Hahhhhhhhhhhhhhh!!"

That alone led to Selen grabbing the crystal and throwing it at the window.

There was a crash as it smashed through the pane, landing outside, and a scream as it hit someone in the street. Assault charges pending.

"Wh-what's going on, Selen?"

"Sorry, Lloyd, I thought I spotted a type of insect I cannot abide."

Her forceful dialogue cancellation left the fortune-teller cringing.

"Selen Hemein!"

"Damn, Selen!"

"Do not concern yourself. I apologize for the abruptness. But if I see another insect like that, I may wind up with my hands wrapped around the fortune-teller's skull."

Threats spilled out of her without reservation. The target of them quivered, despite her rank advantage.

"Can't wait to hear the results! I heard 'ten,' but I'm certain that couldn't be ten percent. You merely misspoke."

Choline shuddered. "Who browbeats a fortune-teller for a good answer?"

It was like she was rerolling a phone game.

"It matters not, the path I choose, but the effort I put into making it work. I am merely taking your advice!"

A wild misinterpretation of her superior's well-intentioned platitude. Yandere stalkers sure put a lot of effort into the exact wrong direction.

"Let's try this again."

The fortune-teller gave Merthophan and Choline a plaintive look.

Choline gave her a *go on and lie* look. The fortune-teller nodded in fast-forward and made a show of reexamining her check sheets.

"Gosh, my mistake, I totally missed this part."

"My, my! That explains it. Eh-heh-heh."

"Oh, and this part. It should be this, right?"

"Eh-heh-heh. True! My mistake."

"Mind if I pretend your birthday is something else?"

"Go ahead! It can be anything you like today."

Selen was making the most of her second chance. And the fortune-teller's leading questions were adjusting things so their compatibility was much improved.

All her espionage spies engaged, trying to locate the right answer.

"If the birthday is here...and we reverse this..."

Few things speak more to the sanctity of human life than a willingness to adjust birthdates. You could make a whole documentary about that.

And the final result...

"Okay! Got it! Lloyd and Selen are...drumroll, please...one hundred percent compatible! Thunderous applause."

"My! I can't believe it. We'll have to get married!"

The match was rigged.

Her soul mate (LOL) Lloyd was busy fixing the window she'd broken, bending the nails straight, fusing wood to wood with the strength of his grip—not how *humans* did carpentry.

"Um, Selen?"

"Ohhhh, Sir Lloyd!"

"I know you're scared of bugs," he said, smiling. "But you can't start throwing and breaking things."

"Um, our compatibility..."

"I picked up the crystal, too, and didn't see anyone on the ground, so that yelp must have been my imagination. But what if you *had* hit someone and hurt them? As the head of the first-years, I've got to be firm on these things."

"Um, right. I'm sorry."

"And allow me to apologize to the fortune-teller as well. You can have this back."

He held out the crystal, bowing his head. Selen and Vritra followed suit.

Choline and Merthophan were looking rather proud.

"He's certainly grown a lot since we first met."

"Yep. Got a bit of confidence, starting to get a sense of his own strength."

Selen, however, looked crestfallen.

"I should have corrected the compatibility in a less destructive manner. I regret it."

Her future was alarming, and both older officers looked concerned.

But what about the man who yelped when he got crystal walloped? He was lying down, some distance from the scene.

"I was completely hidden! How could she have known I was there?"

Once again, it was Zalko.

To quickly summarize: He'd followed Lloyd here on the assumption he knew where the real king was, and the man he'd shared an important-sounding conversation with—Merthophan—had joined them. They had staggered their arrivals—at a stall run by an active duty spy!

He was sure now. Whatever was going down in there was *vital* information.

In full stealth mode, he crept around back, ear pressed against the window, listening in. As the tone grew grim, he took a quick look inside—and Selen's ultimate attack, Take a Hint Crystal Toss, hit him right in the face.

"She must have spotted me…and instantly threw that crystal. But she didn't come after me, so that was merely a warning? No…they're letting me roam free?"

It was just Selen's usual madness, but paranoia was strong with this thief, and he was taking everything to the worst outcome.

"I won't be defeated so easily, Azami! My reputation as a thief depends on it! I'll make this kingnapping a success and fulfill my client's goals!"

The Azami army had unwittingly earned themselves a grudge.

Furiously, Zalko pressed some ice to his brow, trying to soothe the lump.

Meanwhile, Lloyd's group emerged, checking the time.

"We've gotta find that statue."

"The one from Profen?"

"Yep. You look, too, Merthophan. And if you spot anyone suspicious, they might be this Zalko thief in disguise."

"Got it. I'll let Nexamic know. Wish we could have looked around together longer!"

"M-Merthophan, do you mean…?"

"Lately, I'm slow on the uptake with anything unagricultural. Your explanations are invaluable! I feel that if I don't study non-farm things, it'll impact my field performance."

"I feel like there's other things you should study…"

"Oh? For example?"

"Lov—well, if telling you worked, I wouldn't be in this fix."

They wandered off—happy in their own ways.

"Lloyd, a moment," Vritra called out. It had been a while since the belt had spoken to him directly, so Lloyd immediately looked nervous.

"Um, yes? Can I help you?"

"I just wanted to confirm that it was you who removed the Holy Sword."

"Holy Sword? No, I just picked up a rusty old blade that was stuck in the hill behind the Village of the Holy Sword."

That's the Holy Sword, bro. Vritra was tempted to tell him, but decided the ensuing argument would be a distraction.

"Ah…and that is the ace up our sleeves."

Lloyd had no idea what that meant.

"You've grown in confidence. I've been watching you from my Mistress's—from Selen's—side. I can tell. Compare yourself from when we first fought to you now—it feels like there's a rock-solid core beneath that surface."

"Th-thank you."

"Look after Alka. She may be a lust-filled leprechaun now, but she was once as wise as they get. No matter what happens in the future, I asked that you alone remain her ally—gah!"

Before he could say any more, Selen gave him a hard yank. "Don't leave me out of it, Vritra!"

"S-Selen...Mistress, men must exchange words in private at times."

"That sounds tantalizing!"

At this juncture, a big man in a maid dress slid into her vision.

"There you are, Belt Princess! I knew you'd be with Lloyd!"

"Blegh, Allan! How dare you soil my sight with yourself!"

"You're the one who left the shop mid-shift! You don't even realize how hard it is for a man to wear these things!"

"I have been searching for the statue with Sir Lloyd while scoping out some other stalls."

"Oh? And your next destination?"

"Somewhere dark, away from prying eyes."

He glared at her. "Everyone's pissed. Get back to work."

"Selen, I'll handle the search," Lloyd volunteered.

"Very well! I'll shall be waiting for your return, Sir Lloyd! Forever, if need be!"

Always ready to do what he asked, she raced off toward the café... leaving two men in maid drag behind. There was an uncomfortable silence.

"Any luck finding the statue or your uniform, Lloyd?"

"I checked the lost and found, and they said they'd let me know if anyone turned it in. How are things at the statue search headquarters?"

Allan shook his head. "No progress. Rol's getting cranky, since we haven't even found a glimmer of a clue."

"Oh dear. Well, this thief is famous for a reason. Where could he have hidden it?"

"He's only human! Given the time frame, it must be in the Central District. And we will find it!"

Blissfully unaware that their beloved Alka was the true culprit, they exchanged manly nods.

"I'm going to go check anywhere I haven't already. Let me know if anything comes up."

"Got it. I'll handle the shop…gah!"

Mid-chest puff, Allan looked horrified and hid himself behind a pillar.

"Mm? Allan?"

"Shhh! Lloyd, shhh!" He desperately put his finger to his lips.

Curious, Lloyd turned around and saw…

"'Sup, Lloyd. Haven't seen you since the rite."

The leader of the Ascorbic Domain, Anzu Kyounin.

A master of the blade, she wore the distinctive garb of the Domain and a large *tachi* at her hip. As her nation's leader, she'd appeared in countless magazines, and even in Azami, passersby recognized her.

"N-nice to see you again, Lady Anzu." Lloyd bowed, maid skirts swaying. They looked so good on him Anzu stifled a laugh.

"I dunno what stall that's for, but you sure go all out."

"Ah-ha-ha, I've been hearing that a lot. You're here to see the king, too?"

She scratched her head. "I didn't really have set business, but…she insisted."

Anzu jerked her thumb over her shoulder. A beautiful black-haired woman in a red dress stood behind her.

"Nice to see you, Lloyd."

She bowed elegantly. This was Renge Audoc, leader of the Domain's Audoc clan.

"You came, too, Lady Renge?"

"An elegant arrival, naturally… Why that outfit?"

"Um, we're running a café. Ah-ha-ha."

"I shall ask no more. I assume it is training to build your confidence in…many things. But both this happily married woman and this sad spinster Anzu can attest to your strength."

"Aw, I've still got a lot to learn," Lloyd said dismissively.

Anzu, meanwhile, was glaring at Renge. "I can attest to his strength, sure, but really? Sad spinster? We're going there?"

"Heh-heh. You may be our ruler, but I can sense the desperation."

"I always figured you were only contesting my rule to get a leg up on me somehow."

"That is but one of several reasons. More importantly…"

Renge turned toward Lloyd, her voice quiet but powerful.

"Where might Allan be?"

Perhaps an explanation is in order. The Ascorbic Domain held a regular competition for the right to rule—the Sacred Mountain Rite. For a string of reasons, Allan had ended up on Renge Audoc's side. When the tournament wrapped up early, he'd agreed to help fill time—and she'd demanded his hand in marriage and promptly held the ceremony. She was now legitimately his wife.

Having reluctantly accepted his request to wait until his graduation, she was left dreaming of the newlywed life to come...and had tagged along with Anzu as an excuse to see him. One of those "I was in the neighborhood!" scenarios.

Oblivious to all of this, Lloyd was on the verge of telling her Allan's location—hiding right behind him. But...

"*Hngg...*" When he looked, the male maid's eyes were begging him not to.

So he feigned ignorance.

"Um, good question...sorry!"

"No prob," Anzu said. "Surprise visit and all. And Renge—even if you see him today, you'll just have to part immediately. Won't that just make it worse?"

"True," Renge said, drooping. "A fair point, Anzu. That's why I'm here for other reasons."

"Oh? First I've heard of it. What reasons would these be?"

"Allan said a marriage certificate would be inappropriate while he was still a student."

"He did."

"So all he has to do is drop out of school and we can live happily ever after! I'm here to raise objections to his current life and browbeat him into abandoning it."

She did not mince words; even auditors on a mission to drastically reduce personnel expenses were not so blunt.

"So she's gonna make up a reason to drag Allan back with her," Anzu said with a sigh. "Love makes us crazy, I guess."

Behind the pillar, Allan looked terrified. He was suddenly teetering on the precipice of fate. Concerned about the impact on his life and the statue search, Allan sent Lloyd another secret eye contact missive.

"Lloyd! If you mention the statue, Renge will disrupt the search! Keep it secret!"

"I see! They're both highly skilled, and you think I should ask them for help!"

Sadly, Lloyd had not read Allan's message loud or clear.

Allan let out a silent shriek. No blood was left in his face.

"Nooooooo! Don't say a woooord!"

Meanwhile, Lloyd's behavior was arousing suspicion...and he was totally lost, unable to figure out Allan's intent. For a moment, they got stuck like that—then a forty-something individual upended everything.

"Mwa-ha-ha! I make a supply run and hear familiar voices! If it isn't my eternal allies Anzu and Renge!"

"Ugh, Nexamic."

"Inelegant even in foreign realms."

But Tiger Nexamic was not a man to care if he was welcome.

He looked at each in turn and jumped right in. "Consulting about the case?" he asked. "Mwa-ha-ha! Do not leave me out! I've heard the news myself and am already assisting!"

"Case?" Renge said.

Nexamic's muscles bulged, his tongue wagging away. "You haven't heard? Profen's statue was stolen! Allan might be expelled because of it!"

Allan. Renge jumped at that word.

"Spill them beans, Tiger."

"Whoops, Renge! Your accent's slipping!"

"Quit beatin' aroun' the bush and get yer jibber-jabber on! Allan might be what?!"

Nexamic must have felt a chill, because his glutes quivered mightily, and he quickly explained everything.

Renge nodded slowly and firmly. Then...

"I see it now! This is how our life together begins!" she bellowed.

"What ails you, Renge?"

"If Allan is discharged, he'll *have* to move in with me! Our marriage can truly begin! It's *ideal*."

"B-but...think how Allan feels!"

"That's a shame, Lloyd. But I ain't lettin' my hubby get away. Once the dust has settled, he can reenlist if he wants! But first, I'm gonna find this dang statue, smash it to bits, and secure my wedded bliss with my own two hands! Whoo-hoo!"

You can't just drop in and out of the army like it's a part-time job.

Renge was in full hustle mode, all trace of elegance forgotten, ready to let her lust drive her—and it was up to Lloyd to talk her down.

"You can't do that. Do you want Allan to lose his job?"

"Fiddlesticks, Lloyd! Unemployment is all the rage these days. I can't wait to have him dependent on me! A husband's crisis is a wife's opportunity!"

Her full-bore accent just made this all the more terrifying. Needless to say, this was all the exact opposite of elegant.

"You're going full Selen here..."

Three cheers for the birth of a new yandere! ...Nobody? Okay.

They say one man's fault is another's lesson, and "full Selen" was definitely a fault big enough to snap Renge back to reality.

"......I—I am? That bad?"

"Yeah, and...the accent thing's not working out."

Even Nexamic was trying to talk her down.

"I—I can't apologize enough. It seems thoughts of Allan are driving me to distraction. I'd better have some tea and collect myself."

She produced a pot from...somewhere and began pouring tea directly into her mouth. That was more like negative elegant...

"Renge," Lloyd insisted, "I get wanting to be with those you love, but I think there are limits!"

All three of them looked surprised by the strength of his tone.

"Allan has a dream of his own! He wants to be a great soldier and make his father proud. You should be supporting that goal, Renge. What kind of wife ruins her husband's dreams?"

His sincerity was really getting through to her.

She squirmed a moment, then smiled. "You're so much more confi-dent, Lloyd...and that was a most elegant lecture."

"I may be dressed like this, but I'm the head of the first-years."

"And responsibility made you step up," Anzu muttered. "As the Domain's leader, I could learn a thing or two from you."

She smiled like her little brother was all grown up. Renge nodded in agreement.

Meanwhile, Allan was still hiding behind that pillar, tears in his eyes—probably just pleased to have his self-appointed "master" speak this highly of him.

"Very well, Lloyd. I'll settle for a single glimpse of him today and then elegantly help search for this statue."

"You promise you won't try to make him quit?"

She nodded. "I accept that he has his own goals in life and will do my part to assist with them."

Looking relieved, Lloyd immediately turned to the pillar.

"Hear that, Allan?" he called.

"What? He's here?!"

Allan sheepishly emerged from hiding. "Sorry, Renge."

"Oh, Allan..." She gasped.

"I know I've done you wrong," he said, letting his feelings pour out. "The whole marriage thing just got my head all turned around...and I needed time. And I had so much I wanted to learn here in Azami, at Lloyd's side... Can you wait a little longer? I swear, I've never once had a problem with you."

He was being dead serious. Like a romantic confession.

And Renge...was frowning pretty hard.

"You look *hideous.*"

"Ah!"

He had completely forgotten that he was in maid drag. A mistake that could not be dismissed as comic. Here he was, out of sight in a distant land, forced to do god-knows-what! That would earn him a horrified look or two.

"Allan, you cannot stay here. They are defiling you," she spat. She grabbed his hand and tried to pull him away.

"R-Renge! Wait a sec..."

"No excuses! You're confined to the Domain for an elegance re-education! Twenty-four hours of common sense drills and tea-soaking!"

"W-wait, what happened to assisting me? To letting me do what I want?"

"Allan, that means you were listening this whole time. Eavesdropping is not elegant! And what you want is bad drag?! Removing you from this bad influence is the only solution!"

"You were always gonna take me back to the Domain no matter what, huh? Look, I know this outfit sucks! Put the ax down! Augh, help!"

In drag, Allan ran away, crying. Renge went after him like a thing possessed, a hatchet in each hand.

Swing! Swing! Slice!

Like he had a slasher hot on his heels, Allan took big strides, heedless of how his skirts were flying up and revealing his (men's) underwear at every turn.

This horrifying spectacle was making Renge even more livid, and she started using her secret clan arts.

"Secret art—Dragonfly!"

Her hatchet flew from her hand, arcing through the air, attacking anything and everything in its path. Not a move you used on a husband, really.

Two axes screeched through the air in all directions. One touch of either blade spelled doom, their razor edges slicing all and sundry.

There was a small shriek along the way, but Renge never broke stride.

"Hellllp!"

"Be elegant and allow yourself to be captured, Allan!"

They were soon out of sight.

Anzu and Nexamic stood staring after the sad escape scene.

"Mwa-ha-ha! To be young again, Anzu!"

"I'd rather stay old, Nexamic," Anzu said, shaking her head.

With Allan gone, Lloyd was at a loss. "Um, what now?" he wondered.

Then, a new soldier appeared. "What's all the fuss? This part of the case, Lloyd Belladonna?"

"Oh, you're the head of security! No, nothing to do with it. It's just Allan—so he'll be fine."

Lloyd saluted. The man before him had been in the statue briefing, representing the security department.

"Allan... Well, if he's headed toward the source of the commotion, I'm sure it'll soon be resolved."

"Oh...ah-ha-ha..."

Unable to admit that Allan had been the cause, he settled for an awkward laugh.

"I'm sure it's just some fool getting carried away. But our army places too great a burden on young Allan's shoulders. I've heard the locust disaster would have been far worse had he not been there."

That was mostly cleaned up by Lloyd, with some help from Alka's meteors. Allan had done his best!

The security chief sighed, grumbling, "At times like this, whether our security team has combat experience makes all the difference. Like everyone in the Ascorbic Domain—I frequently wish we could get instructions from them regularly."

The "fool getting carried away" was from the Domain—and the lead of the Audoc clan.

"Domain training?" Lloyd asked.

"Yes." The security chief nodded. "Our cadets are getting solid training from Colonel Chrome and ex-Colonel Merthophan. But the ranks before they stepped in largely graduated without practical experience. We're forced to pound it into them on the job."

"Gosh."

Lloyd was trying to find an opening to point to Anzu and Nexamic, but the security head's flow didn't allow it.

"The king arranged for you to receive hands-on instruction once, yes? It needn't be anyone on Lady Anzu's level, but I would love to have a first-rate instructor in residence here. Sadly, most qualified people who leave the Domain end up working as bodyguards for the rich, or with the guilds."

"A first-rate Domain instructor, hmm?"

"Yes, an Ascorbian master, as close to Lady Anzu's level as we can... mm?"

Realizing that Anzu herself was standing before him, he momentarily locked up. Not having meant to startle him, she scratched her cheek, then introduced herself.

"Hi, I'm Anzu Kyounin. I happen to be the leader of the Ascorbic Domain."

"————!!!!!!"

He had clearly never been so startled in his life. However, he wasn't head of security for nothing and he soon recovered, returning the greeting.

"...'llo, Azami military security chief..."

His voice took a second to catch up with his tongue, and Anzu looked rather guilty.

An awkward silence settled over them, but Nexamic had never been one to notice these things, and his hamstring flex interrupted it.

"And I am the Domain's own Tiger Nexamic! I've been following the Azami agricultural advisor Merthophan around, learning the ways of the farm!"

This was awkwardness blown away by outlandishness. For once, Anzu was grateful for the sweaty beefcake.

Normally, Nexamic's behavior drew scorn, but here it proved invaluable in helping the security chief recover his aplomb. As disgraceful as blowing a greeting was, *this* man was clearly a living disgrace.

"So I've heard. Have our forces treated you well?"

"Mwa-ha-ha! They are indeed! Did I hear you rabbiting on about Domain instructors?"

"Rabbiting... Oh, you heard that? How awkward. Thing is..."

He proceeded to relate what he'd told Lloyd to the two of them—how his forces could use a good combat instructor and how they'd be happy to offer a residency.

Lloyd listened intently, and when it was over, he offered a suggestion.

"Lady Anzu, do you think Renge would be interested?"

The security chief was shocked to hear Lloyd drop the name of the Domain's premier ax-master so casually.

"Lloyd, mind your manners—"

"Oh! Wonderful idea, Lloyd! She'd be overjoyed!"

"Er…you know each other?"

Before he could even finish chiding Lloyd, Anzu had her arms around the boy.

His expression said, *Are these two BFFs?* And Nexamic responded with a side chest pose.

"Friendship written in muscle! All bonded by the purest of emotions!"

This explained nothing, but the security chief got the gist. He remembered how Lloyd had spoken out against himself, the top diplomat, and the head of public relations.

"Who needs strength when you have the courage of your convictions?" he asked.

"Exactamundo! Aaaaand! Hamstrings!"

All Nexamic's beef bounced in agreement.

The veteran soldier looked Lloyd over once more as Anzu teased him. Then he grinned.

"If you know you're right, then say your piece. That kind of heart is something I—nay, the Azami army—have lost sight of."

Of course, that wasn't even the kid's *real* strength.

Done with Lloyd, Anzu turned back to the security chief and held out her hand, smiling.

"Soldier, I'd be happy to set up that residency. I can send you the chief of the Audoc clan, Renge Audoc."

"Y-you can? A clan chief would come here?"

"Yep, and it won't be some once-a-year thing. She'll likely live here for the foreseeable future."

"Really? A-are you sure…? But a clan chief instructing us would likely cost a pretty penny."

"Doubt that'll be a problem. Give her a solid wage and a place to live and she'll earn her keep."

Seeing the look of disbelief on the man's face, Nexamic boomed, "Go for it, Azami! It's what Renge wants, and Lloyd is already one of us!"

"I'll chat with Renge herself and your king, but I bet it'll all work out. Lloyd, I'll help look for this statue once that's all over."

"Mwa-ha-ha! Me and my pecs have your back, Lloyd! Tiger Good-Bye! Till we meet again!"

Anzu fluttered her fingers and sailed away, Nexamic with her.

That series of rapid twists had left the security chief stunned, but then he turned and grasped Lloyd's hand.

"Thank you, Lloyd! You made this all happen!"

Lloyd was looking rather bowled over.

"I—I didn't do much! I just made a suggestion."

"Your help was invaluable! The way you just speak your mind directly is vital! The soul of Azami!"

Lloyd had never been called the soul of anything before and was having trouble keeping up with his superior's mood swings.

His enthusiastic speech concluded, the security chief asked the question:

"What are your plans for the future?"

"Er, um…not decided yet."

"Then by all means, join the security team! If you gain the skills to match your candor, you'll be a perfect soldier!"

With that equally enthusiastic recruitment, he ran back to the headquarters, medals jangling.

A few minutes earlier, while Renge was chasing Allan away—yep, that shriek was our old pal Zalko.

He'd been purchasing another lump of ice, trying to cool the lump Selen had given him.

"Oww…my head… Daaamn… Mm?"

He'd looked up to find Allan in drag and on the run.

"That's Allan, but…why?"

People around were running, too, and Zalko moved against the flow, hiding behind a pillar, trying to figure out what was going on.

And a flying hatchet shaved the top of his head.

"What the—? Aughhhhh! The whole top of my head! Down to the roots!"

Zalko found himself the proud owner of a reverse mohawk.

First they caused him physical pain, and now a blow to his psyche. Zalko was left teetering on the precipice of despair.

"Shit! Trying to drive me round the bend with a head shave? The humanity! Is that any way for a soldier to behave?! They're animals!"

Zalko had been aggressively pursued any number of times, but this sort of roundabout hazing was genuinely enraging—though of course it was entirely unintentional on their part.

"I'll show them! I'm gonna find this real king and—"

Before he could even say "kidnap," someone gently patted him on the shoulder.

"'Sup, baldy. Got a sec?"

A tanned boy, with a smile—Shouma.

"I'm not bald! I just got my head involuntarily shaved! Urp!"

Mid-rant, a hand clamped down on his throat, shutting him up. The strength was unbelievable. Clearly fatal.

His strangler's smile never wavered. Those eyes *weren't* smiling, however.

Zalko had met his share of killers, but none of their eyes had been this dark. It felt like an icicle stabbed into his heart.

"Wh-wha…?" That was the best he could manage.

"Prying eyes here. Let's move."

He was dragged away by the neck at an unfathomable speed. His vision was blurring, but it felt like he'd blinked and was in a forest.

Literally in the blink of an eye? Am I dreaming? He hoped this wasn't real, but the creaking of his neck bones forced him to conclude otherwise.

This new and horrifying sound was making him quiver like a leaf.

"Whoops, sorry, don't want you staining that uniform. You know that when they hang people it opens all their orifices? Everything comes running out."

Adding to the terror, Shouma dropped Zalko to the ground. As Zalko gasped for air, Shouma stripped the uniform away.

"Yep, Lloyd's uniform… Mm?"

Shouma sniffed the clothes, frowning.

"Ugh, you got that old man smell on 'em! What the hell? You wanna transfer that to the owner?!"

"I… Who…are you?" Zalko rasped, tasting blood in his mouth.

Shouma gave him the kind of look usually reserved for insects. "I'm asking the questions…but your throat's too damaged to speak?"

Once Zalko was down to his T-shirt and underwear, Shouma kicked him hard in the side. Zalko bounded away like a rubber ball, slamming into a tree.

"Nghhh!"

"Now you can't run even if your throat heals." Shouma yanked him up and cast healing magic on his throat.

The broken vertebrae were instantly back to normal, and he could breathe again.

None of this should have been humanly possible, and Zalko was beyond terrified.

He could torture me the rest of my life, and I'd never die.

That thought shredded the last of Zalko's resistance.

Shouma's smile never wavered.

"Question time. Why'd you steal this uniform?"

"……To kidnap the king."

"Oh, I see! Good for sneaking inside. So pure coincidence it was his? Good!"

Zalko had no clue what was good about it.

"Okay, this one's just pure curiosity. Why kidnap the king?"

Zalko didn't give a fig about his secrecy policy here. He spilled all the beans.

And his anger with the Azami military.

Shouma listened raptly. He was especially surprised to find that this man was working for the local lord, who worked for him.

"Well, well, Tramadol sure has rotten luck," he muttered.

"You're not with Azami?" Zalko asked, frowning. "You're not here to finish me off?"

"I'm not Azami—actually, I'm on your side. You just happened to step in it big time. Stealing that uniform is downright cursed! You should probably go see a priest, get that lifted."

Shouma sounded almost sorry for him.

Zalko had no idea how this man could possibly be on his side, but he was too tired to think straight. He was just muttering away, venting his hatred of the Azami army.

"And he's stopped listening… What do I do with him…? Oh!"

Someone was pushing through the trees.

Shouma turned to look and found Sou standing there.

"What's up, Sou? Find what you were looking for?"

"Mm," Sou grunted, holding up some old books.

"Those *are* old. You becoming a reader on me? Or…?"

Sou's lips curled—calm, but sardonic.

"I'll be burning these."

And as he spoke, the books went up in flames. Hardcover volumes were instantly reduced to ash.

Bizarre though this might be, Shouma just seemed to enjoy the show.

"What a shame! You got it in for the author?"

"Not the author, but the character. The hero, Sou—this was a novel based upon my exploits."

"Isn't that nice! Oh, wait, that means…"

"Novels like this spread my tale the world over and trapped me here when my role was done. Buying several copies of the same book earned me strange looks from passersby and the costumed balloon distributor. Vexing."

Sou brushed the ash off his hands as if he were scattering the ashes of a fallen comrade.

"Every little bit raises the odds that I can disappear. Comic, really. A unit I was in for a matter of months, yet our deeds ballooned up in a heroic epic. They've got us fighting with ancient weaponry Dr. Eug built! They say truth is stranger than fiction, but sometimes the opposite is true."

"Huh, that sounds like the book I gave Lloyd…"

"What was that, Shouma?"

"Mm? Oh, nothing."

He had no way of checking, so he decided he didn't care. Sou's attention drifted to the groaning heap of Zalko.

"And your undressed companion?"

"A thief named Zalko. Tried to kidnap the king, bungled it. And had the bad luck to steal Lloyd's uniform, which meant I nabbed him."

"So Lloyd remains in maid garb?"

"He does! And I wanted to get mad footage while it was still light out. Still ain't got a single publishable shot!"

"That's a crying shame. Hmm…"

Sou looked Zalko over. He was just looping through complaints about the Azami army like a broken record.

"Think we could use him, Shouma?"

"This old dude?"

"He's got a grudge against Azami, we need photo ops, and Dr. Eug wants us testing those new demon lord products…"

Shouma snapped his fingers. "Gotcha! We have this dude go on a bender, and Lloyd steps in to save the day! He'll be the hero of the festival!"

He stepped in close, grabbing Zalko's jaw. All smiles.

But his eyes were as mean as his smile wasn't, and Zalko quickly shifted to begging for his life.

"P-please! Don't—"

"Don't worry! We're not gonna kill you. You're gonna be *useful*. Like I said, we're on your side!"

Shouma yanked Zalko's mouth open, pouring in a mystery fluid and some tablets.

Zalko coughed and sputtered, but Shouma made sure the thief swallowed.

"The key here is your instinct for anger and resentment. The stronger those desires are, the better your demon lord compatibility. I'd totally forgotten, but you are pretty good base material! This should be passionate."

"It's starting, Shouma."

Zalko let out a voiceless screech.

"_____"

It felt like fires spreading through him. He rolled around, thrashing—and then went limp.

And a stone coating appeared on him.

Petrification.

Sou looked at Shouma. "What demon lord is this?"

"A golem, I think? Sturdy stone body, super powerful, infinite capacity to heal itself. Oh, already complete! That was quick."

Zalko rose to his feet, reborn in a nine-foot-tall body of stone, his bare skin like a classic sculpture, yet his face twisted with rage.

"*What...is this?!*" Zalko asked, his voice now muffled.

"You've been reborn!" Shouma beamed. "How's *that* for passion?"

"*Reborn?*"

"Yep! See? Let your instincts drive you! No ethics holding you back! Feels good, right?"

"*It does.*"

"We want you wreaking havoc. You hate the Azami army? So show 'em."

"*Azami... Azamiii! They made a fool of me! I've got to teach them a lesson!*"

Growling, Zalko turned his lumbering body and moved away.

Shouma waved good-bye and grinned at Sou. "See? Dude had pep."

"Shouma, there's no time to waste. Give Lloyd back his uniform so he's ready to fight! Get our cameras in position! We must be ready."

Both of them looked pleased as punch, like high school students when the last bell rings.

Demon lord Zalko...well, his stone body was about to cause *more* problems.

Dear readers, I'm sure you know why. He looked *just* like a statue!

Chapter 3

Steam-Powered Payback: Suppose a Dude Blows Your Deal *and* Gets Mad at You for It. You Should Totally Hit Him with a Locomotive.

By this point, Lloyd was looking at Chrome's "Find Who's Hiding" document, trying to figure out where the statue might be hidden, or where Zalko might be lurking.

"They said it was bigger than a grown man, so it should be hard to miss..."

If only he knew what it *looked* like, he thought, moving steadily away from the hubbub.

"They said to make sure the king didn't find out, but we should at least have asked him for a description."

His feet had carried him to the area behind all the stalls.

This zone was full of water barrels for washing dishes and huts set up to keep garbage away from the fairgoers' eyes.

"What's up, Lloyd?" a soldier said, waving to him.

"Oh, hi. I'm looking for the st— Wait."

Lloyd trailed off—that information was top secret.

The soldier didn't ask. He just looked at Lloyd's clothes and assumed he'd run away. "They really did a number on you, huh? Nobody goes back that way, so feel free to take a load off. Nothing back there but an old storehouse."

"That's what I'm looking for—thanks!"

Lloyd bowed his head and followed the soldier's directions. A few minutes later, he found an old storehouse, surrounded by overgrown trees.

The paint was peeling off the walls, and the structure was covered in vines—very well camouflaged.

"Um, this must be the place... Maybe someone's already checked it out, but just in case they missed something, I'd better look inside."

Lloyd opened the door, politely calling out, "Anyone here?"

Light streamed in, illuminating the gloomy interior—all kinds of bric-a-brac, long since abandoned.

"Wow, there's a lot of stuff in here... Urgh, blegh!"

He caught a whiff of something moldy and spluttered. Mid-cough, he spotted something else.

"*Cough, cough...* Mm? Is that...? Oh!"

He'd found the box of butler clothes Zalko had stolen. He opened the lid and found it full of chic butler uniforms.

"Why is it *here*? But this is perfect! I'll just change real quick while nobody's looking."

Lloyd tore off the maid outfit, switching to butler mode. An empty storehouse was perfect for a quick change.

He had been certain no one else was here, but just as he finished changing...

"Mmph! Mmph!"

"Eep!"

...a muffled groan came from the floor, and Lloyd jumped a foot in the air. As he freaked out, something came crawling toward him. He slowly looked down...and found the king tied up, with a gag in his mouth.

"Um..."

Lloyd wasn't sure what that meant.

What? It's like he's been kidnapped, but...is this an act? It must be! Selen said something about an escape trick! That must be it. If he'd been kidnapped, everyone would be in a tizzy!

And thus, yet another poor soul failed to detect the crime in progress.

The king's secret escape practice ended in failure, and he's waiting for rescue? We were told to ignore him...but I can't do that, can I?

With that thought, he smiled, said, "Lemme help you," and reached for the gag. It was like he was helping a cat that had its head stuck in the tissue box again.

"Hngggg!" The king was pleading with him to stop smiling and free him.

Lloyd gently took the gag out, careful not to hurt him.

"Hah…hah…thank you. You're…"

The king went straight into thanking him, ignoring the fact that he'd seen the boy change.

"Not a problem. Should I take the ropes off, too?"

"O-of course!" The king had no clue why that was even a question. The escape trick practice theory had never crossed his mind.

Free at last, he stretched his back (with an audible *crack*) and then flexed his wrists (which was followed by more popping).

Finally, he took a deep breath and said, "You've saved me. I've been like this all day!"

"Really? Oh, dear. That sounds bad!"

"Well…I nearly gave up a few times. Especially when people saw me like this and just left me here! Why would they do that?" He looked rather sad.

Lloyd remembered an important question.

"Oh, right! I should ask you."

"Mm? I'm sure you have many questions! You see, I was kidnapped by—"

"What's the statue look like?"

"Is that relevant?!"

Lloyd seemed utterly uninterested in the kidnapping, and the king was starting to suspect something more was afoot.

"This boy's the same as those girls earlier… Do you not *know* I've been kidnapped? No, you must! I'm the king!"

He had no way of knowing that was exactly the situation.

"Well, we should get you checked out. Let me help you to the infirmary," Lloyd said, and tried to escort him out.

THUD. The noise was pretty far off—but it sounded like something flipping over.

"What the…?"

"What was that?!"

They looked at each other. With the king leaning on one of his shoulders, Lloyd made haste toward the commotion.

Meanwhile, back at the combination maid-and-butler café and statue search headquarters…

As the café business boomed, Rol was growing more and more frustrated in back.

"I never imagined we'd go this long without so much as a hint of a clue!"

There were detailed maps of the castle and campus areas on the board, both gradually getting covered in red check marks.

The majority of the Central District had been investigated. It might be time to broaden the search area—perhaps the culprit and statue were *outside* the district. That was bad news: They'd never meet their deadline. And that had Rol on edge.

"No good, Rol?"

"I've searched everywhere I could think, but…found nothing."

Choline and Merthophan added their checks to the map.

"You *did* search thoroughly, right?" Rol said, scowling at them. "Nobody's gonna laugh if you were too busy flirting to notice."

Choline turned bright red. "Heck no! We wouldn't! We didn't…flirt! And this statue's bigger than a man! You can't overlook that!"

"You suuuure? Ugh, I just can't believe we've searched this far and found zilch."

There was a hint of panic in her voice, so Tiger Nexamic popped his pecs in return. "Mwa-ha-ha! My Tiger Hamstring Dash took me from corner to corner with no statues in sight!"

"And I sure didn't think you'd let *this* guy tag along…"

"I'm with you there, Rol."

Nexamic's presence was certainly drawing puzzled looks, a favor he returned with a double bicep pose.

"My elegant pursuit of Allan took me all over, but no suspicious behavior or statues were to be found."

Once Renge had captured Allan and forced him to change back into his uniform, she'd tied him up and was using him in lieu of a chair, elegantly sipping tea. Everyone was trying not to look.

"So that's Allan's wife?"

"That goes *beyond* whipped."'

"Total domination."

She was *literally* sitting on him, to the horror of every man present.

"You could have just said this was the costume for a maid café," she grumbled.

"If I'd have stopped to talk, you'd have killed me, Renge."

Laughing at this close couple conversation, Anzu turned to Rol with a suggestion. "I've heard the news, ma'am. I'm Anzu Kyounin, leader of the Ascorbic Domain. If you need help, my blade is yours."

"Well, that is an honor. What brings you here?"

Rol bowed politely, but Anzu waved a hand, dispensing with formalities.

"Lloyd helped me out before. We can certainly hunt statues for you, but frankly, we're better in a fight than in a search party."

Nexamic and Renge both nodded in agreement.

"For Brother Merthophan and Lloyd, this tiger will skin itself!"

"Peel off any more layers and you'll wind up in the slammer. But my husband dotes on this Lloyd boy, so I shall cooperate. Elegantly!"

As the three Ascorbians stepped up, a booming voice echoed from the back.

"Seeee?! If our Ascorbian brethren are in, then Rokujou's Sardin will not stand idly by!"

"Ugh, the dumb dandy—I mean, King Sardin!" Rol said, forcing a smile, her voice rather clenched.

Sardin approached, all smiles—but his eyes narrowed at the sight of her.

"I believe we've met before," he said. "Weren't you formerly the headmaster of Rokujou Sorcery Academy? I owe you an apology. I wish I could have offered more help when you were being led around by the rot of our society."

That rot had almost wrested control of his kingdom from him, and he felt responsible for all their misdeeds.

Despite his reputation for frivolity, the man before her clearly had his wits about him, and Rol quickly matched his speed.

"Mena and Phyllo briefed me on your situation. I'm sure you had it far worse than I did. Especially because of their use of necromancy— arts I personally developed." She glanced meaningfully at Sardin's wife.

Ubi reached out and shook her hand. "Ubi Quinone," she said, her tone friendly. "Certainly, necromancy complicated things, but...I'm not holding that against you. No need to dwell on the past any further."

"That is a huge relief, I'll admit. I'm sorry for everything."

Rol bowed her head, and Riho slapped her on the back.

"Nice, Rol! You got yourself pardoned!"

"I imagine I owe Lloyd for that one, too."

Mena and Phyllo finished marking up the map and joined them.

"The dumb dandy will be of no use, so ignore him—but don't worry, I'll make up for it."

"......Have him help serve tea."

Daughters versus fathers, a war that never ends. Sardin proved to have absolutely no defenses and was instantly sobbing into his wife's sleeve, all trace of wisdom gone.

"Augh, Ubi!"

"Shut up and get pouring."

Neither his two daughters nor his wife showed him a shred of mercy; what a shame. This bickering was creating quite a stir.

"Not surprised Phyllo doesn't even give a king an inch."

"Or Mena."

"They made him cry!"

"Is it me, or are they all a lot alike?"

They'd been keeping their relationship a secret, and in the interests of maintaining their secret, Mena quickly changed the subject.

"So where's Lloyd got to? If you let him wander around in maid clothes, some weirdo might take him home."

"Mwa-ha-ha, little lady! Indeed, Lloyd was far too adorable, but no one could restrain him against his will! Speaking of adorable, behold the Tiger Nexamic hamstrings!"

"...Coming from a weirdo, not convincing."

Sardin and Ubi were growing somewhat concerned about their daughter's increasingly eccentric social circles.

Renge felt Allan shift under her and addressed him. "The ever-elegant Lloyd is so powerful that he can literally fly, so I'm sure no harm will befall him. Right, Allan?"

"I completely agree."

One Ascorbian constantly flexing, the other mounting her husband in public.

"Just to be clear," Anzu said, "They're considered nuts back home, too."

Firmly placing herself on the side of sane.

Watching all this were the diplomatic liaison and security chief, as well as the PR rep—having finally recovered from his kebab-flavored soft-serve-mandated trip to the toilet.

"Hmm...everyone's talking about Lloyd. He's friendly with the Ascorbic Domain leadership? He'd be an invaluable asset to the diplomacy branch!"

"Another feat earned by his sincerity. Sounds like he knows the king of Rokujou, too. I'd love him to join the security team, and to train him to be my successor."

"Everyone loves a cute face! He'd be the perfect new mascot for our army! The royalties on merch alone would have the money rolling in!"

The PR dude was getting kinda grubby.

Rol noticed her superiors had returned and had gotten the conversation back on track, looking the map over as she addressed the room.

"Okay! We may not have found the statue, but Zalko himself has got to be waiting within earshot. We've got international help now, so let's keep our spirits up and see this through."

""""Aye-aye!"""""

As cries went up all around, she scowled at the check-covered map.

"The statue and Zalko... Lloyd isn't back yet, but unless he found something..."

Then a soldier came bursting in, out of breath. "Excuse me! Urgent message!"

"What? You find it? The statue, or Zalko?!" Chrome asked, closing in.

The man nodded. "The former, sir! We've found the statue!"

A cheer went up, but the messenger looked rather grim.

Sensing something amiss, Rol asked, "Where was it? Is there a problem?"

"Th-the statue...it's, uh..."

He caught his breath and spoke loudly enough for everyone to hear.

"It's in the central square! Wreaking havoc in the train and carriage display!"

Azami Kingdom. Central District. Main square.

Watched over by a (slightly beautified) statue of the king, this was where Lloyd and the other cadets had taken their entrance exams.

The Military Festival was using this square to display the trains from the cross-continental railroad, as well as the army's cannons—and the triumphal parade wound through it.

And the stone demon lord—Zalko—was leaning against the king's statue, roaring.

"_____"

It wasn't every day that a nine-foot-tall moving rock started silently screaming at you.

The crowd soon realized this was not part of the show and quickly grew alarmed. Zalko stomped his foot like an angry toddler, and the train flipped over. The ground shook from the impact.

This was *real*—and the crowd scattered like spiders.

The search for the stolen statue meant that security had been beefed up, so there were soon nets and barricades surrounding the area and a line of communication opened to headquarters.

Rol led a group of soldiers in, gaping at the spectacle.

"Why is the statue attacking?!"

It wasn't actually *the* statue, just a demon lord made of stone, but...it was the right size and had chosen the right day, and—

"No wonder we couldn't find it! It was moving on its own!"

"Zalko the Thief...what a nasty trick! A most elegant foe."

"I'd heard the statue was rather abstract, but it's pretty simple! Perhaps that gives it depth? It certainly speaks of love. As the head of the second-years, I can tell."

Lots of convenient interpreting was going on, but none of them doubted that this demon lord was the Statue of Love on loan from Profen.

The moment Selen spotted it, she immediately abandoned teamwork, trying to bind it in place.

"If I catch it, then Lloyd is mine! Right, Phyllo?"

"...Ah, no fair!"

"Cry me a river!" Selen yelled. Yandere always attack first! Phyllo was a step behind, but Selen was already barking orders to her belt. "Vritra, bind!"

"Right away! Hi-yah!"

"Selen! It's a loaner! Don't break it!" Riho yelled, spotting their bosses in a tizzy.

"Don't worry! I know how to—"

But the statue dodged the belt's bind with alacrity, backhanding it as it did.

"Huh?"

"......It's rather skilled!"

The statue hadn't *looked* nimble. Vritra sounded quite impressed.

Seeing the startled looks on the assembled soldiers, the stone demon lord chuckled.

"An attack like that can't capture Zalko the Thief!"

""""Zalko?!"""" everyone gasped.

"He got us good!" Rol swore. "That explains it! He's got a power that lets him possess objects! He took over the statue and kept it on the move, avoiding detection! The spell might have a lot in common with my necromancy."

Without any doubt that this demon lord was the Profen statue, this explanation seemed plausible. That kind of mutant power had never really been a thing before, though...

Perhaps they'd have worked out the flaws in their logic if they'd had time to think things through, but with limited information and everything going on—nobody was really inclined to do that.

"......You showed yourself before we caught up with you?"

"Exactly, Phyllo. He knew we wouldn't dare harm the statue, so he possessed it—a brilliant plan. Damn!"

Phyllo and Mena were left hovering at the sidelines, unable to step in.

"If it's strong enough to knock Selen's belt aside… But my katana would definitely damage it. Capturing this unharmed won't be easy…"

Ubi, Sardin, Nexamic, and Renge were busy helping evacuate civilians—none of them could see a way to help with the capture.

"Dear me…there's no chance to extend my loincloth!"

Merthophan was already stripped down again but couldn't find the appropriate opening. That phrasing sounds pretty bad, but not as bad as it would look!

The upperclassmen were particularly frozen—harming this would ruin their future prospects. The bosses were all but screaming, "Don't break it!"

And right in the center of all this chaos…was Marie, here to enjoy the festival.

"What's going on? What kind of show is this?"

Micona spotted her and pounced. "Ahhhhhhhhhhh! Marie!"

"Wha, Micona? Seriously, what is this? Is that *the* statue?"

Micona, ready to pounce at a split second's notice, paid *this* no attention and just gazed at Marie, enraptured, possibly damaging her future prospects.

"Yes! The matchmaking statue!"

"Does matchmaking usually involve rampages? Are we sure this is the Statue of Love…augh!"

She made a lot of sense, but Zalko's next move drowned her out.

"Rahhhh! Diieeeee!"

As if venting all his steam, Zalko punched the train. A wheel flew off, burying itself in the ground nearby.

"Tch! It's too dangerous here. Someone could get hurt!"

"But we can't hurt *it*. What now?"

No options. They were at an impasse.

Then…

"Dammit," Allan swore, stepping forward.

"Wait, Allan!" onlookers said, but he brushed them off.

"Stop that, Zalko!" he roared. "I'm the one you want!"

"Hngg?" Zalko turned, looking down at the little man below him.

Allan flinched, but steeled his nerves and kept yelling.

"Listen up, sneak thief! Knock this off! You want me out of the army so you can flaunt it to the Lidocaines and all of Azami, right?"

"......*What?*"

"Fine, then! I'll quit if I have to!"

"Allan?!" Chrome gasped. "Why?!"

Allan turned back a moment. "I don't want anyone getting hurt on my behalf. And this is a good chance to reset my rep back to what I actually deserve."

Then he turned toward Renge.

"A-Allan...," she said.

"I might be out of a job, but will that be a problem for you?"

"No. I'll love you all the more."

Roses were in the air. Everyone sighed. If the situation had been less tense, they might have clapped. Surtr—possessing the ax at his hip—muttered, "Show-off." But even he was clearly grinning.

Allan put on his game face and fixed the stone demon lord with a glare.

"Give the statue back. I'm pretty pissed off here—but go, take a swing. Toughness is my middle name!"

He turned his cheek, waiting.

But Zalko didn't seem very interested. *"Honestly? I don't even care."*

"Huh?"

"It's the king of Azami I hate! Him and his army!"

"Wait a sec—this whole thing was *your* idea! Now you're just blowing my chance to act like a badass?"

"Arghhhhhhhhhh! They made a fool out of me! Azami can burn in hell, hell, hell!"

He was losing control of this possession.

"Ah! Look out! People, move away!"

Marie's leg cramped up and she toppled over. That dang rune curse...

"Hnggaah! Guhhh!"

She face-planted with a most undignified noise.

"Hahhh! A hostaaage!"

As everyone else ran, Zalko scooped her up.

"Marie, you dumbass! I told you to get your exercise!" Riho yelled.

"That's not it!" Marie wailed. "Okay, I don't exercise, but arghh… that kid grandma!"

Zalko held Marie high, bellowing, *"See?! I have a civilian hostage! If you don't want her crushed, bring out the real king!"*

"What's this about a real king?" Rol asked, baffled, as well she might be. Zalko was in a realm of rage only achievable through stupendous bad luck.

But when the demon lord's captive "civilian" was the princess in disguise…that complicated things.

First off, Micona blew her top the moment she saw her beloved in peril.

"Marieeee! Curse you, Zalko! I'm gonna shatter your ass!"

Both her treant and Abaddon powers activated as one, rocketing her into combat mode—and the students around her were forced to try to hold her down.

"Wait, Micona! If you startle him, her life—you've gotta wait for the right moment!"

"That's right, Micona," Choline said. "You saw how it stopped Selen! If you run in alone, the worst could happen!"

"Right!" The PR guy nodded. "The statue might get hurt! That would be the worst!"

"…Somebody shut that old man up."

Even Phyllo looked visibly revolted.

"A civilian death would be tragic…but if the statue's destroyed…"

"We'd all be forced to resign. Is there a way to save *both*, Rol?"

The security and diplomat heads both turned to Rol, hoping for ideas. The word "resign" definitely had her swearing.

"Civilians' lives have to take priority…but a way to save both…"

The threat to her career made her flinch, and she couldn't bring herself to give the order to attack.

Then…

"What's going?" A boy's voice carried over the square.

Everyone turned his way—and found a boy in butler clothes, the king leaning on his shoulder.

Chrome took one look at Lloyd, saw the king covered in dirt, and ran over.

"Wh-what happened, Your Majesty?"

Having been kidnapped so easily, the king looked remorseful.

"Sorry, Chrome. I made you worry again."

"Oh, I wasn't worried. But why are you so dirty?"

"Why *aren't* you worried?!"

Not one soldier here was aware that any kidnapping had taken place. Chrome himself was just assuming the king had tripped or something.

And this treatment was really starting to make the king fume.

"I was kidnapped, and not one of you cares—mm? What's with this statue?"

Before the king could get a good look at the stone demon lord, the three military bigwigs formed an iron defensive wall, obscuring his line of sight.

"Your Majesty! Your robes are a sight! Allow me to clean them for you!"

"No, that statue looks—"

"Your Majesty, allow me to wipe your face!"

"And is that Maria…? Mmph!"

"Your Majesty! Lemme just—"

"Where are you wiping?! That's not dirty!"

As the soldiers swarmed them, Lloyd looked horrified.

"! Marie?! What *is* this?"

"Calm down, Lloyd. You see, Zalko—" Mena quickly filled him in.

Lloyd looked shocked, then nodded. "Okay. What a cowardly plan!"

And immediately, he stepped out before Zalko.

"S-stop!" The PR guy gasped. "What can *you* do?"

Lloyd paid him no attention. "Let her go!" he howled. "I-I'll be your hostage instead!"

Zalko's eyes widened. *"You?"*

"Yes! So let her go! Or are you scared of me?"

A desperate ploy.

Zalko let out a derisive chuckle.

"Scared? Hardly. I just love seeing Azami soldiers at their wits' end!"

"Wh-what? Why?"

"You made a fool out of me, so I'm gonna make a fool out of you! I'll show you what happens when you mock the great thief, Zalko! All I ever wanted was fame and attention! To prove wrong all those people who said my face was forgettable!"

"And *that's* why you stole the statue...and took Marie hostage?"

The air shook.

Riho, Chrome, Anzu—anyone who could detect Lloyd's power— flinched.

Lloyd's eyes narrowed. "You're a *bad* man."

"Yeah! I'm a thief! Of course I'm the bad guy!"

Zalko chose to own it.

And Lloyd clenched his fists.

"How awful."

Alarmed, the PR guy tried to talk him down. "Boy, I admire the motivation! But if you harm that statue, you're fired!"

Absolutely the wrong thing to say here. The security and diplomat chiefs both slapped the back of his head.

"Harm the statue...and you're fired."

Lloyd heard these words and tore the first-year head armband off his sleeve, tossing it to Allan.

"L-Lloyd?"

"The rest is yours, Allan. Take care of everyone."

"Meaning...what? Huh?"

Lloyd took another step forward, right up to Zalko, and yelled as loudly as he could.

"I enlisted to help people! If I can't even save the people I care about—then I don't *want* to be a soldier!"

"What? Are you angry?"

"I am."

"But what will your anger accomplish, little boy?"

A feeble-looking boy against a massive statue.

He didn't stand a chance. The security chief began barking orders.

"You there! Stop him!"

As he panicked, Riho grinned.

"Once he gets going, nobody can stop him," she said. "And don't even think about saving that statue. It's done for!"

"Not my concern!" the security chief roared, aghast. "The boy's about to get himself killed! We can't let that happen! Nobody exemplifies the Azami army spirit better than he does! He's honest and sincere! That's the kind of boy our country's future depends on!"

"Exactly!" the top diplomat agreed. "We all got caught up jostling for position and forgot ourselves! That boy is who I used to be! We've gotta... Why is everyone so calm?"

Everyone who knew Lloyd's strength was certain he'd win.

"...It's doomed."

"Yes, I would gladly trade places with Marie."

"Geez, Belt Princess, can't even drop that act for one second?"

"I would rather be in Lloyd Belladonna's place!"

Chrome stepped over to the three bigwigs, looking confident.

"Just you watch," he said. "He's the pride of our army. A true soldier."

But between taking in Lloyd's goofy costume and sass, Zalko was reaching new heights of fury.

"You dare lecture me dressed like that?! Die! Die! You have to die! I'll crush this woman—"

Pssht.

"Hngg?"

A glint.

And it was over.

A wind come out of nowhere—

"M-my hand?! It's gone!"

—and sliced through Zalko's wrist.

It was like someone had swung a sledgehammer and broken it clean off.

"What are you gonna crush her *with*?"

A *very* calm voice came from above. Zalko's stone head creaked as he looked up.

Against the cloudless blue sky was Lloyd, hovering in the air, holding Marie, as well as Zalko's hand. The scene was like something out of a religious painting.

"Flying?! My hand! Why? So fast?! How?!"

Zalko was speaking in fragments, his mind unable to keep up.

Lloyd peeled Zalko's hand off Marie, one finger at a time, each shattering into dust, which flitted through the air below them.

"Does it hurt anywhere, Marie?"

"N-no…"

Marie had never seen him like this.

"Micona!" Lloyd called, dropping down to her level. He handed Marie over. "Take care of Marie."

Micona took her like a child would a birthday present.

"Nice pass! You got it, Lloyd Belladonna!"

"And once I've left the academy, look after the rest of my class for me."

"Hmph, I suppose I could grant a final request."

Lloyd gave her a smile as strong as it was sad and flew back up to Zalko.

"What are you?! Are you even human?! How are you flying? Aero? That's insane!"

Nobody else used *Aero* to hover. Although nobody else used demon lord power to turn themselves into a stone giant, so…

"Normal response." Anzu chuckled, scratching her head. "Basically what I said."

"Lloyd's improving so fast! I never imagined he could fly!" Sardin gushed, pulling his sunglasses down to get a better look.

"Having actually fought him…I'm lucky to be alive," Ubi said, sweating.

10/10 reactions from the royal couple.

"Oh! This is a trick! You still dare mock me, Azami army?!"

Forgetting he no longer had a hand, Zalko took an angry swing… and found himself pinned to the ground like a moth, his arm twisted behind his back.

The impact was so great that the ground split beneath him. Lloyd wasn't even using both hands.

"You didn't even put your back into it," Lloyd said. "If I can stop it one-handed, you clearly haven't trained hard enough."

"*Hah?!*"

"I've always been weak! But I found a good master! I trained at the holy grounds in the Ascorbic Domain! I worked hard! And now I can fight like this!"

Lloyd released his arm, *Aero* slipstreaming past it to kick Zalko hard in the side.

"Mwa-ha-ha! But of course! Lloyd always had the potential, so a visit to our lands unleashed it all! One could say my muscles brought him to this point!"

"I have no idea why you're claiming credit when you didn't do a thing. Although I am tempted to do so myself—elegantly, of course."

Nexamic and Renge both beamed at Lloyd like a favorite nephew.

"Geez," Anzu muttered. "Crediting us when the one who really trained him was Satan, a passing demon lord… Whatever makes him happy, I guess."

She was grinning just like her compatriots. The only person not grinning was poor Zalko.

He was experiencing an all-new form of terror reserved for those who've been hit so hard their body cracks.

"*Gahhh!*"

Flung aside, he tried—midair—to recover his balance and catch himself, but before he could hit the nearest building—

"Not done yet!"

Lloyd got there first, kicking Zalko's bulk again before he could slam into the wall.

With a dull *thunk*, the statue rocketed upward…like a beanbag.

And that high up, he had no way of avoiding Lloyd's wrath.

"Next…"

Crack! Lloyd's fist shattered one of Zalko's legs.

"Before you hit the ground…"

Snap! He spun, using the motion to karate chop the other leg off.

"…I'm gonna reduce you…"

Bam!

The other arm, shattered with a head-butt!

"...to rubble!"

Bam! Crack! Wham! Thnnnk! Pow, pow, pow!

Lloyd's *Aero*-enhanced flutter was a full-on barrage.

Like he was being torn apart by birds of prey in the air, Zalko himself stayed suspended, chunks and pieces of him torn off and pulverized until—

THUD.

His head and torso alone hit the ground.

"Oh...oh...oh..." Zalko was just sobbing now.

As Lloyd landed, his fist shattered Zalko's torso, too. No one had ever seen him look this angry.

"I've left you the head. Use it to repent."

Lloyd had completely destroyed this hideous monster, and the audience was left speechless with awe.

But those who already knew his skills quickly started a round of applause.

"Wow!"

"Who is that butler?"

"He can fly?!"

The cadets were frothing. For those outside his inner circle, this was their first chance to see what he could really do.

"I always figured Lloyd was good, but this good?"

"Amazing! Our whole class are monsters!"

"Goddamn," Riho said, laughing. "He finally did it in front of everyone! Nobody can argue with this one, Lloyd."

"Oh dear...he's going to have so many fans! But I have a lock on the role of first wife."

"......He's more confident... Now he just needs...self-awareness. Several kinds."

With Zalko defeated, Lloyd had made a beeline for Marie.

"Marie, are you okay? No injuries?"

"N-no. Just...a leg cramp..."

Lloyd looked relieved. And then he bowed his head.

"I'm sorry. I've gone and destroyed the Profen statue. Now I'll be

©Nao Watanuki

expelled from military school. You've been such a big help to me, it's a shame to end it like this."

"But you did it for me," she said. "Don't look sad. I'll come apologize with you. As the princess of this kingdom."

"Marie, this is hardly the time for jokes."

They both laughed, but Marie's laughter was definitely a touch desperate. How could she make him believe her?

"Don't flirt when I'm watching...," Micona growled, clearly the worse for wear; this display of romcom shenanigans had left her crying tears of blood.

Meanwhile, the king was watching Lloyd and Marie, his eyes wide.

His daughter was clearly in love with the boy in the butler uniform.

"......That's the boy who lives with Marie and helps her with housework, right? But...he's so strong? Did I have the wrong idea?"

He'd finally worked out that Marie was in love with Lloyd, not Allan—and it was this boy who'd saved him from Abaddon.

"Allan's feats were so dizzying I never realized... Aha! So it's this boy."

The king attempted to approach...

""""Your Majesty!""""

...and his path was once again blocked by the three military head honchos, all bowing low.

The security chief raised his head first.

"Sorry, Your Majesty. The theft of the Profen statue and this entire situation is my responsibility. I shoulder all the blame—none lies on that boy!"

The diplomat joined him. "No, this is a failure of diplomacy and our relations with Profen Kingdom. I will take full responsibility, so please—our armies need that boy! He's the perfect soldier!"

Finally, the PR boss bowed his head. "The two of them accept all responsibility! Let that boy remain a soldier. Our PR campaign needs someone that cute *and* powerful!"

""""What the—?!""""

Fists grabbed his shirt from both sides.

"I mean...I haven't paid back the loan on my house, so..."

The king watched their routine a moment, then sighed. "Gentle-men," he said. "I would never fire that boy. Why is this even being discussed?"

"Well...we begged Profen to loan us the Statue of Love, and he just pulverized it..."

"Mm?" The king glanced over at Zalko's head. "That's not the Pro-fen statue. The real one isn't anything that simple; it's far more com-plex and bizarre. Avant-garde."

""""""Huh?!"""""""

Even Rol got in on that one.

"Th-then what was it?"

"Don't ask me!"

The shattered fragments of Zalko's body were collecting themselves around him.

Within moments, he had his arms and legs back.

"Ha! Bwa-ha-ha! Your luck's run out! The power of the stone demon lord makes me immortal!"

"Stone...demon lord?"

"Exactly! Quaking in your boots? Bow before—!"

"You—"

"Yes?"

"You're so confusing!"

Zalko's mess had been entirely unrelated.

Every cadet there, along with the international guests, all unleashed their strongest blows, turning their frustration into a total romper stomp.

"Er? Wha...why? I could dodge all this easily before? You mean you were all holding back?!"

"Of course we were!"

"...But not anymore."

"We're laying on the hurt till you can't regenerate!"

"You will *pay* for hurting Marie! And the ensuing emotional turmoil."

It was an all-out attack. A brutal beating that made Lloyd's barrage look adorable by comparison.

"Back off a second and let me hit him with a big one!"

Riho had gone to the train tech display and loaded up the locomotive with coal.

It was a hybrid magic stone and coal train and had luckily been left unharmed by Zalko's rampage. Between the coal and Riho's mithril arm's magic enhancing powers, it was now on the move. Only she could pull that off.

"Y-you're kidding..." Zalko looked horrified, and Riho had never looked more evil.

"Stay right where you are! You've done major harm to our maid café! So much profit, flushed away!"

That sounded pretty personal. She sounded the train whistle.

No one moved to stop her. The train lurched into motion, speaking for everyone there.

"Drop dead, asshole!"

"Only supervillains use trains as weapons! Aughhhh!"

The train hurtled out of the display, right toward Zalko—

Chugga-chugga-WHAM! Whir, whir, whir.

The train hit him hard and was knocked on its side, wheels spinning away. A grisly sight. Zalko was pulverized again, pieces of him falling like rain, a sight to make any human flinch.

And this crowd of civilians was definitely starting to get scared. Can't blame 'em.

"Wh-what in the...?"

Rol grabbed the magic voice amplifier, quickly covering. "Th-thank you all for coming! This is...the Azami army's centerpiece performance! A d-demonstration of our might! An endurance test for the new train! Work out the rest for yourselves!"

The train was pretty smashed up, so if this was a test, it probably hadn't passed.

The crowd's reaction was mixed.

"I figured! Real impressive."

"Pretty risky, though..."

"They really went all out!"

"This military might will protect you all! We love our citizens!" Rol had both arms out, gesticulating and sweating buckets.

Riho gave her a look of pity, but clearly, hitting Zalko with the train had improved her mood immensely.

"Ha-ha, trying to spin this chaos… Never want to get promoted into a job like that."

She heard a citizen mutter, "Love for Azami is terrifying," and winced.

Once the full team beating was over and everyone felt better—

After crumbling and reforming again and again, even with the demon lord's power, Zalko was helpless to stop Lloyd and the others from demolishing him. At last, his will to fight had given out, and he reverted to human form.

Chrome apprehended him, looking confused.

"So where is the real statue?"

"S-statue?" Marie asked.

"It was stolen, and we just caught the crook."

"O-oh…a statue, you say? Mm…why does that remind me of something…?"

"Do you know where it is?" Lloyd asked.

"Um…I dunno how you could call it a Statue of Love." She frowned. "Maybe…something to ward off evil?"

Go on and cry, Alka.

While Marie made funny noises, the soldiers closed in on Zalko for questioning.

"We'll just have to pry the information out of this thief. Good work, Lloyd!" Rol exclaimed, doing her part as search leader.

"R-Rol!" A soldier ran up to her.

"What?" she asked, looking cross. "We're busy laying the hurt on a crook until he spills the beans on the statue's location."

"W-we may have found the statue! I-it's back in the treasure room!"

""""Whaaat?!"""""

This was so sudden it just confused everyone. The king and Marie had never understood anything and were extra baffled.

As everyone looked for answers, Satan came in, dragging Alka by her collar.

"Such a stupid thing to hide. See, Alka? It's a huge deal."

"It's not stupid! You can't tell me you don't have any secrets in your closet!"

"I do, but I'd handle them without getting the whole nation into an uproar."

They were bickering like children, but there was an ominous vibe under those words.

"Hey there, Chief Alka, Satan," Riho called out. "You mentioned hiding a thing..."

"We didn't," Alka lied, clearly wanting no part of this.

"Yeah, Riho, you see..."

"Traitor!" Alka snapped, but Satan ignored her and explained both what she'd done and why.

Everyone who knew how nuts Alka was just found this punch line depressing.

"I would rather not have known..."

"......She's the chief of troublemaking."

"We should have started by listing who could easily access our treasure rooms..."

This was all hitting Alka hard, and she turned to Lloyd for comfort.

"Wahhh, Lloyd, they're being mean!"

Lloyd dodged her tackle—a clear act of rejection. "Repent, Chief."

"*Gasp!* Lloyd? So harsh!"

"You need to repent."

Alka's soul appeared to leave her body. She was like...an old woman being scolded by her favorite grandson.

Just as it seemed like everything was settled, Chrome's brow furrowed.

"But then what did Zalko steal? Was it all fake? Concerning."

".........."

"What's wrong, Your Majesty?"

"...Oh, nothing. Bringing it up now would ruin the mood."

There was no bigger wet blanket than telling people you'd been kidnapped. This was a rare instance of the king employing tact. He resolved to take it to his grave.

Instead, he made his way to Marie's side.

"Maria, you're unharmed?"

"Y-yes, just a spot of bad luck, Dad."

"And after I asked you to come... I'm afraid the festival feature I prepared for you is a bit of a mess now. All I managed to do was give you a fright."

Marie looked taken aback, but soon gave him a reassuring smile.

"Don't worry about it. I appreciate the thought. And..."

She glanced Lloyd's way, her smile growing.

"...I got some thrills all my own." She remembered how mad he'd been when he came to save her, and she blushed.

The king was definitely in fussy dad mode.

"So he's the one? If I'd noticed any later, I'd have summoned Allan to an audience and Maria would have killed me..."

"Mm? Dad, what was that?"

"Oh, just thinking out loud. Mm?"

As he shook off his prior mistake, Sardin and Anzu approached.

"Hello, King Azami! It's been too long. I must thank you again for helping save Rokujou!"

"Oh, King Sardin. The pleasure was all mine."

"Lloyd in particular was invaluable. And—oh, is this Princess Maria? Hmm?"

"Ah-ha-ha, we meet again. It's been too long."

She looked guilty, having failed to introduce herself in Rokujou. She'd spent her time there making sure Lloyd was dressed nicely and generally reveling in hedonism.

Sardin's wife joined the conversation.

"It was a chaotic time. I'm his wife, Ubi. Your Majesty's actions have allowed me to be with my husband once more."

She bowed her head, and the Azami king did the whole *please, raise your head* routine.

Then it was Anzu's turn. "You didn't figure her out till now, dumb dandy? I knew pretty early on."

"Ah, Lady Anzu. I suppose I'm no match for feminine instincts!"

Sardin would usually manage a snarky word or two in response, and Anzu looked rather surprised to find his tone sincere.

"You seem far less on edge than at the conference. I'm guessing he saved you, too?" she asked.

"Too? Lady Anzu, you mean…?"

"Yeah, some gnarly forces were trying to wrest control of the Domain, but thanks to Lloyd, we managed to stop it in time. Gotta say thanks again, King Azami."

Accolades from two fellow rulers again made the Azami king elevate his estimation of Lloyd Belladonna.

The boy himself was flanked by the security, diplomat, and PR heads, looking bewildered.

All of them had been so caught up in their positions and passing the buck—and now they were bowing their heads to him.

"He's every bit as talented as the Dragon Slayer," the king muttered. "Perhaps more so! Lloyd Belladonna… Well, if he wants it, I could arrange status worthy of my daughter's hand."

As he muttered to himself, his fellow rulers began moving on.

"Come, King Azami. We've got a parade to view."

"Right! Gotta show yourself in good health, right? I know we've got lots to catch up on, but that's gotta be your top priority. Where have you been all day anyway?"

"Ho-ho-ho! That would be telling."

The king laughed it off, glanced once more at Lloyd, then headed happily back to the castle.

The second Shouma recovered Lloyd's uniform, he'd gotten his cameras set up and had cheerfully filmed Lloyd's entire fight with Zalko. He looked as pleased as a housewife fresh from a sale.

"Beautiful footage! An all-out battle in butler garb! Passion radiating everywhere! I was really worried when he was stuck in maid clothes, but as long as the climax lands, it's all good! Right? I'll slip his uniform back to him later."

He was checking over the footage on the camera's playback screen, smiles spilling over.

"Passion! Passion! This footage is hot, hot, hot! Perfect Lloyd heroism! No one can argue with it! This alone would make a movie!"

At this point, he stopped himself, shaking his head. "Wait, wait," he muttered. He started pacing back and forth. "I *really* wanna show everyone, but...we've gotta get the timing right! Unleash demon lords the world over, have Lloyd defeat them! And *then*...!"

Shouma swung around, beaming at the sight of Lloyd with the military top brass.

"Passion! He's got his bosses on his side, paving the way for more stardom!"

As his enthusiasm reached a fever pitch, Sou appeared, looking far more downcast.

"Yo, my man, Sou! What's up? You're even gloomier than usual."

"Shouma... It's nothing, really."

Shouma frowned at this, but was too eager to show off his footage to dwell on it.

"Well, I've got footage that'll cheer you right up! Lloyd totally strutting his stuff! We've just gotta prep a bunch of villains for him and place the world in peril! Then he'll save everyone, be a hero, and be happy! And so will I! And so will the world! A passionate finale! And the final boss will be you, Sou! And at the perfect timing, we'll unleash this footage on the world! Once everyone knows beyond a doubt that Lloyd saved them—you'll finally vanish!"

Sou barely seemed to hear a word.

"...Yes...he'll be the new hero, and I'll be gone. And to prevent me from being dragged back into being, make sure the footage is clear. Sou is evil; Lloyd is good."

And with that, he began walking away.

Shouma stared after him, puzzled.

"What got into him? Can't believe Lloyd's combat scene didn't put a smile on his face. But then again, if death's staring you in the face...I suppose you would get emotional!"

But even he seemed to know this explanation was a little forced.

The reasons for Sou's mood...had occurred a few minutes earlier.

"Wazzup, good sir. I can't tell if you're a middle-aged hottie or a gray fox, but we gots to talk."

Sou slowly turned around. Even in the hubbub of the Military Festival, this voice was jarring.

He found himself face-to-face with a rabbit costume. Its hands were full of balloons.

The adorable pink fuzz was certainly festive, but it was so *deeply* cutesy it looped back around to "creepy." Perhaps "inhuman."

"State your business," he said, undaunted.

The rabbit stepped forward, clown shoes squeaking.

"Here I was, handing out balloons, and I saw the most fascinating thing! A man buying a bunch of copies of the same novel and then hauling them off into the woods. What for?!"

"To burn."

"Let it burn! Burn! Buuuuurn!" The rabbit did a campfire dance. The occupant had clearly known the answer all along.

Sou let a beat hang, then asked, "What do I look like to you?"

The rabbit pretended to consider this. "An old friend."

"Oh?" Sou said. Clearly an unexpected answer.

"Let's walk and talk. Sou the sinister. The runeman. Even a bunny costume would look ordinary at your side, yes? You've got that knack for making people perceive you that way."

"You know much about me."

They began walking, both automatically heading away from the crowds.

When they reached a deserted alley, the rabbit bowed.

"I apologize for the late introduction. I'm Eve Profen, king of the same named land."

Sou did not bat an eye. "Profen's ruler… That is of no concern. Only a handful know I am a runeman. Meaning—"

"Yep, yep, same generation as Alka and Eug."

"It is surprising that Profen is ruled by one of you…but what do you *want*? Something you can't simply pass to me through your friend Eug?"

Eve did a happy dance. "I've got valuable intel for your ears only! Good thing I decided to go undercover here in case you stopped by."

"Intel? But there is only one matter I care about."

"Exactly! A way to guarantee your end."

Sou's eyes were like daggers.

Eve kept babbling away, not the least bit perturbed. "You just have to kill Lloyd Belladonna!"

"I have little sense of humor."

The gleam in his eyes was intense.

Eve maintained a light, comedic tone, explaining, "Alka and Eug told me all about you, so I looked into it. You've been unstable for ages. But ten years ago, you developed a clear consciousness."

"Yes, that's when my thoughts and feelings began to return. And I began to lament my inability to die."

He uttered this like a curse, to Eve's evident delight.

"Ten years ago, a boy happened to read a book. And the soldier in that book inspired the boy to travel here, to Azami."

"——!" Sou gasped, connecting the dots.

"That boy's name is Lloyd Belladonna. The same boy you're 'passionately' trying to prop up as the new hero."

"...Wait...if that's true, then..."

"It is," Eve said. "Ancient runes...complex symbolic letters. Once fused with what we call 'magic,' they allow the manifestation of our imaginations. In our day, we called them the new age runes, or rune treatment. You had no clear mind of your own because you'd run out of magic and the imagination that gives it form. But what currently gives you shape is Lloyd's own immense magic reserves and the way his admiration of the soldier in the novel inspired his imagination."

"But...there's no need to kill him. If he killed me..."

"That would be tricky. He perceived you as a bad guy, right?"

"Yes. That's why he is fit to be the new hero."

"Quite the opposite. He perceived you as a bad guy because your actions are in opposition to his conception of hero. The moment he kills you, you'll revive—as the hero he desires."

This was just Eve's interpretation.

However, it hit a little too close to home. It felt real to him.

"Thanks," he muttered, and he turned on his heel, vanishing back into the crowds.

Eve watched him go, swaying with delight.

"Yes, if you kill him, I'm sure Alka will team up with us to bring him back to life!"

She didn't care if Sou vanished or was trapped in this world for all eternity.

Eve acted only for her own goals, without a trace of guilt about the consequences.

With the festival concluded, normalcy was returning to the Azami Military Academy.

Cadets and teachers alike occasionally found forgotten flags hanging somewhere, or popped balloons on the ground, and smiled.

As Lloyd helped with cleanup, he thought back on the uproar of the statue case.

Zalko and Alka… Between the thief and the monster, he'd had no time to enjoy the festival itself. When it was all over, they'd dragged themselves back home—but even that was a fond memory now.

"It was hard work…but I'll never forget it."

As for Zalko, he was in prison, getting asked a *lot* of questions. The beating had certainly left him disinclined to be chatty, and they were only getting bits and pieces out of him between long vacant stares. Chrome said it would likely take a long time.

As for the Statue of Love (*pfft*) at the heart of all this, it was sent back to Profen unscathed, to the great relief of the military bigwigs. Everyone demanded to know why Alka had done that, and Lloyd had been so mad at her she'd refused to get out of bed for three days. So her heart wasn't really "unscathed."

"The chief and her weird whims… You forced me to run all around in the most embarrassing clothes…"

Lloyd had certainly suffered, but the rewards were probably worth it.

"Morning, Lloyd! Picking up litter? Impressive."

"Good morning, um…oh, the lady from intelligence!"

"Ah-ha-ha, didn't recognize me without the fortune-teller costume? You want more fortunes read, ask me anytime! I can help with your love life, future plans, anything at all."

People from other divisions often stopped by to chat now. His social circles had really expanded, which was certainly a good thing.

As he watched his spy senior walk away, he muttered, "My future… I've really got to give that some thought."

He'd left Kunlun with only one thought in his mind—to become a soldier like the hero in his favorite novel. That was a pretty broad goal. He needed to narrow that down, find something more specific.

"Mm, right. I'm leading my class! I've got to be a model for everyone. And that means I need a real plan."

They would soon be in the back half of their first year. Determined to figure out the best placement for himself, he flung open the classroom door.

"Good morning!" he said, beaming brightly.

But the first thing he saw was Riho, flat out on the desk, cheeks wet with tears.

"Wh-what's wrong, Riho?!"

Lloyd ran over to her. Selen and Phyllo were already behind her, patting her back. Clearly whatever had happened was dire.

"You were in such high spirits, even after everything that happened!"

Everyone had been exhausted and dragging their feet—but Riho had been as happy as a lark—because the maid-and-butler café had pulled in a small fortune.

"…Mmph," she groaned, not managing to move her mouth enough for it to be intelligible. An old woman with no dentures would probably have better enunciation.

Selen answered for her.

"All the money Riho made from the maid café…paid for the repairs to the train she weaponized."

"Oh."

Lloyd had forgotten all about that. Riho had gotten so angry she'd stolen a train from the display and had hit Zalko with it.

"...Rol said, 'We covered the outstanding balance, so consider yourself lucky.' But...we can safely assume Riho's pockets are empty."

"Nobody stopped her... Frankly, they were all totally into it. So I sympathize with her frustration."

Selen and Phyllo were both poking Riho now.

"I hate you both," Riho croaked. That was all she could muster.

Just as she seemed ready to drown in despair, Allan came in, already raising a fuss.

"Ahhh, good morning, Lloyd! Girls!"

".....Lumping us together?" Phyllo hissed.

"What now, Allan?" Selen demanded. "Have you fled aggressive police questioning like me?"

"Course not," he said, wiping the sweat off his hands. "Only you have that problem. Mine is far worse."

He shivered. What could this be...? Before anyone could answer, the door flew in once more, and in came Renge—in an Azami military uniform.

It seemed she'd pounced on that instructor-in-residence offer and had moved to Azami to be with her beloved Allan.

"Allan, are you *certain* you have a handkerchief with you? And you must make sure to hydrate early. I'll fetch you some hot water!"

"R-Renge! No need to fuss over every... And don't sneak into my room in the morning!"

She was totally playing the unwanted spouse trope to the hilt—which some would probably envy. But she seemed less like a doting wife than his mother.

He looked less than pleased by her fussy flurry.

"My platonic ideal," Selen murmured.

"...She's *too* worried. She's just mothering him now."

Phyllo was much less impressed.

As Renge's mom mode crested, Chrome and Choline came in, looking rather sorry.

"Pardon me, Renge. Homeroom's about to start, so..."

"Oh, dear me. That would not be elegant. I have my duties as an instructor, so I'll dispatch those with grace. Oh, and Allan, study hard and graduate with honors. If you attempt to stave off our happy home by getting held back a year…there will be consequences."

"Eep!"

That last thing was definitely a threat, and Allan's shriek was very real.

"Reconfirming a promise of life together first thing in the morning… What could be better?"

"…A promise *without* a threat?"

Phyllo's deadpan had not crumpled at all, but her tone was clearly disgusted.

"Take care of my husband, everyone!" Renge said, curtsied, and was gone.

"Gosh, you sure picked a winner," Choline said. "But since she's come all the way from the Ascorbic Domain, we've gotta treat her right…and frankly, I could take a few pointers from her bold moves."

That last part was a sigh and a bit too revealing.

"But she's better than Selen. Any problems arise, we can make Allan handle them."

"Yep, it's like she comes with an instruction book! It all goes tits up, we bring in Allan."

"That sounds so ominous."

They both ignored Allan completely, taking their places at the podium.

"Okay, everyone's here? Physically, at least. I see a few minds haven't joined us…"

While Riho and Allan might have been wallowing in blues (financial and marital, respectively), homeroom must go on.

Choline started handing out pages. "Lemme know if there aren't enough."

At the top of the page was written *Career Survey*. Lloyd had *just* been thinking about his future, too.

"N-now?" he asked. The timing was unnerving.

"Yep," Choline said. "Like it says at the top, we want to know what *you* want. Put your preferences in order. You can tell us what you think you'd be best at, or tell us what you've always wanted to do. Don't overthink it."

Overthinking things was what Lloyd did.

Having secured a seat next to him, Selen raised her hand.

"We're only halfway through the school year. Isn't it a little early for this? I heard the upperclassmen didn't start to worry about it until the start of their second year."

"Mm…," Chrome said, making a face. "Well, no reason *not* to think on it."

Phyllo gave him a look of deep suspicion.

Their teachers were doing their best to smile and nod their way through this, but they quickly moved to the corner, conferring.

"What now, Chrome? They're onto us!"

"But we can't tell them the truth! I mean…"

They both looked at Lloyd.

"That this is just because the king wants to give *him* the post he deserves."

"Yeah, on the assumption he'll marry Princess Maria… If Selen finds out, there'll be entrails everywhere."

Forces were clearly at work here.

Unaware of this, Lloyd had his chin in his hand, frowning at the page.

"He's being so serious about it… I feel so sorry for him…"

"But it might work out for us."

"Wait, is there something I don't know?"

Chrome nodded. "All three of those bigwigs are mad for him now. 'Bring him to security!' 'Convince him to be a diplomat!' 'We need him to be our new mascot!' But if they know what *he* wants, maybe they'll resign themselves."

"Right…"

They both glanced at Lloyd again.

"My future… I'll have to talk to Marie once I get home," Lloyd said, sounding his age.

He did not look like the future king of Azami. And he himself had no idea that was in the cards.

Suppose a princess in disguise fell for a kid from the boonies, who wound up ruling alongside her… Nobody would ever think that cliché would happen to them.

Afterword

Fateful encounters happen surprisingly close at hand.

I never thought all this would happen in a few short years.

Shame and a weird sort of pride got in my way, and I shielded my eyes from my feelings and the truth I was aware of all along. In hindsight, I was only embarrassing myself.

But a real man moves past these things. He ignores his own failings and pompously tells everyone this: What matters is courage. I can say now, with pride—I'm glad we met.

…This is all to say, at long last, I have purchased anti-thinning shampoo.

It's got some sort of nifty chemical in it that's definitely reduced the number of hairs lost in the shower, and I'm going, "Why didn't I buy this sooner?!"

With shame, I remember saying, "Aw, it's just spot baldness again. The anime thing *is* stressful." Averting my eyes from the truth! A few years back, I was sure I could make it, but I was a fool! I should have bought the shampoo the first time I saw it on the shelf.

Not to change the subject, but how *do* you meet your soul mate? I've heard life is the greatest game, so is there a button I can press? I don't see one, but is that a bug, God?

*   *   *

Oh, hi, everyone. I'm Satou, still riding that post-shower high from the *lack* of lost hair from my new shampoo. If I'd switched to it sooner, I could have introduced it to any number of follicular friends, but alas...

Before this tangent continues, I'd better dispense with the formalities.

To my editor, Maizou, I realize my first draft was cleaner this time, but the corrections were a mess. I'm sorry.

To my illustrator, Nao Watanuki. Both maid and butler Lloyd are flawless—thank you so much.

To my manga adaptor, Hajime Fusemachi, hats off to the wonderful work in every issue.

To the spin-off artist, Souchu, thanks for making my boy Lloyd look so cute.

To the anime staff, I'm sorry the source writer is such a mess. You all understand the work so well, and I've lost count of how many times I've said, "What, really?"

To editorial and marketing, rights management, retail relations, and everyone else involved with the series—I can't thank you enough. And to all my readers—thank you for reading this series. I hope you've laughed and had fun.

—Toshio Satou

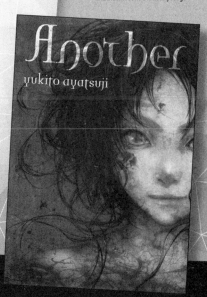